PRAGUE TRIPTYCH

INTERIOR OF CAFÉ ARCO

Johannes Urzidil

PRAGUE TRIPTYCH

Translated from the German by
DAVID BURNETT

TWISTED SPOON PRESS
PRAGUE
2026

ISBN: 978-80-88628-06-4
ISBN: 978-80-88628-39-2 (E-BOOK)

This publication has been supported by a grant from the Federal Ministry for Housing, Arts, Culture, Media and Sport of the Republic of Austria.

Federal Ministry
Housing, Arts, Culture,
Media and Sport
Republic of Austria

CONTENTS

PREDELLA

A Relief of the City

High above Prague, in the Gothic Cathedral of Saint Vitus, there hovers between the pillars of the presbytery a large wooden relief depicting the flight of the Winter King. With troops, horses and carriages he hastens across Charles Bridge, ancient even then, ignobly surrendering the winter throne and his questionable crown to his Imperial vanquisher. As a child I avidly contemplated this carving, not on account of the historical event, portrayed in a rather theatrical manner, but because it was a thrilling tableau of the city: the castle on the hill, the many buildings, the river and bridge, the roofs, gables, cupolas and towers. The vast city, whose warren of baroque streets the boy had often ventured through, passing between the palaces of great Bohemian noblemen and the burgher houses adorned with colorful coats of arms, climbing all the way up to the castle square and cathedral — huddled here on a narrow panel of wood, grainy and darkened with age, was a concentrate of this city. I could experience it as a unified whole, as if it were a person — not to mention the dramatic events, the escape taking place on the bridge — and I could dream up things on my own not depicted by the relief. The dreams of a boy are fertile. They expanded the city for me, as the mind of a young artist would have it.

Heady events like the flight of the king were nothing extraordinary in the history of this city. The city not only survived them, it was almost as if it needed them to survive. The imperial capital of Vienna was considered gemütlich, but the Imperial and Royal city of Prague was anything but, neither on the outside nor on the inside; it was jagged, harsh, pugnacious and uncanny. It may have been wonderfully exciting and a wondrous thing to live there, but easygoing it was not. Ever since the mythical Princess Libuše had prophesied the future glory of Prague from the banks of the Moldau on Vyšehrad Hill, conflict and strife had been endemic there: massive quarrels between the granite boyars of early Czech history as epically, Homerically portrayed by Stifter in *Witiko*; malicious feuds between Czechs and Germans ever since the days of Přemyslid rule; intolerable pressures on the Jewish community, which had maintained its sanctuaries in Prague since the tenth century; violent and bloody religious clashes between Hussites and Papists; religious turmoil and feudal wars between Bohemian noblemen; torture and persecution of the pious Bohemian Brethren, even by a king of their own nation; and unceasingly, as far back as the memories of individuals and nations reach, struggles with the emperor, struggles with German compatriots and neighbors, mutual injustices, no doubt about it, all very hard to untangle.

The boy consulted the history books and came to his own conclusions. "Protestant Bohemian rebels threw the two Catholic imperial governors, Counts Martinice and Slavata, along with their private secretary, Fabricius, out the castle window and into the moat." That's what it said in his history textbook. It wasn't clear to him who was thrown out first, the counts or the private secretary, but it seemed that the defenestration of the secretary was something of an afterthought. Whatever the case, the event marked the start of the Thirty Years' War, or at least its prelude, which directly led to the catastrophe and pitiful flight of the short-lived Winter King.

But the boy, for his part, was still wondering about that "along with." It seemed to be one of those indispensable auxiliary words reflecting a certain approach to history and life, much like the word "only." "No one was injured when Charles Bridge collapsed in the early morning. Only a baker's apprentice, out delivering bread rolls, fell into the river and drowned." That's what the newspaper said. Private secretaries and baker's apprentices existed "along with," were "no one," and "only" died. But even apart from social syntax, hatred and discord continued to find their toxic nourishment in the countryside and capital since the Thirty Years' War. Czechs and Germans mutually abused each other, both abused the Jews, while the imperial nobility was none too impressed by any of them and, in turn, were held in low esteem by the Czechs who, for all their subservience — or perhaps because of it — utterly loathed them. There were always exceptions, of course, but if you focus too much on those you overlook the essence of things and end up losing the proper balance.

How could you expect this city, with all its many antagonisms, *not* to be jagged, harsh and uncanny in its architecture and countenance? Too many different temperaments were running riot there. And however much it smelled of good heavy beer and smoked meats in every street, the clouds of myth hung everywhere: the Golem ran nightly around the Old-New Synagogue, in the midst of the Old Jewish Cemetery High Rabbi Loew held court with his thirty-three favorite pupils buried in a circle around him, Tycho Brahe's golden nose peeked from the crypt in Týn Church, the ghostly houses of the alchemists whispered in Golden Lane behind the castle where the Fausts of the Rudolphine renaissance conjured up gold and spirits — Kafka, too, conjured his spirits and bucket rider there — Dalibor played violin in his tower cell or played with homemade cards — the castellan still waved an ace of clubs painted with the blood of the opera hero — the intact body of the Blessed Maria Electa was well preserved in the glass case of the Discalced, just like the intact tongue of Saint John of Nepomuk in the cathedral, and even more impressively Saint Wilgefortis (known in these parts as Saint Starosta), her full beard protecting her virginity over in the Loreta cloister, and down in the catacombs of the Carmelite nuns the imperial general of the Thirty Years' War, Don Marradas, made famous by Schiller and dried-up like a stockfish, in accordance with the principle: "Old soldiers never die, they just turn into stockfish." Myths, history and the present actively intermingled in this city, you could never entirely tell them apart, you never knew exactly what you were dealing with, and in this strained atmosphere the most trivial of objects, matters, even mere words could at any moment transform into the most sacred goods, for the sake of which Czechs and Germans would bash each other's heads in or rough up some hapless Jew.

It was at least fortunate that the boy did not grow up in a

sheltered upper-middle-class household, in a protected family circle with parlormaids and governesses. Because he got around a lot, no one paid him any mind, he could choose his boyhood friends and enemies wherever he pleased, and he didn't care if his ball crashed through a Czech, German, Jewish, or Austrian-aristocratic windowpane. "Ich bin *hinternational*!" he used to say, "I'm *behind* the nations, not between or above or below them. Being hinternational allowed him to live more freely, roaming the streets and the covered passageways; he could thumb his nose at Kakitz, the watchman in the Town Park (immortalized in a Werfel poem), and run away, or cheat the *Sesselbaba*, the "chair lady," out of her kreutzer. Up on Žižka Hill, where once the blind Hussite hero had routed the Papal-Imperial forces, he could chisel out Hussite cannonballs embedded in the mortar of the wall, and at the Baumgarten he could take part in hinternational track meets with shot-putting, pole-vaulting and hundred-yard dashes, without any of us ever knowing how long a yard really was. The parks were not for the adults, who went for silly walks there or rode around in fiacres; they belonged to us, the boys, as did the squares and alleyways, the courtyards, the Moldau islands and the bridges, especially in winter, when the bridgemen wore mittens in the bitter cold and it seemed to us the height of amusement to put on an innocent face and hold out the toll kreutzer in our palms, so that — cussing and cursing the Germans and Jews — they struggled to grab the coin with their clumsy, fat, mittened hands.

The boy was no "Little Lord," no well-behaved lad who stayed in his room doing homework, oblivious to the world around him, but a street urchin, a Tom Sawyer, Huck Finn. I knew how people and children lived in the outskirts of Žižkov or Košíře, what they ate if there was something to eat, and what they wouldn't eat when there was nothing on the table. I was conversant in their giant arsenal of curses and insults, which they constantly expanded with an inexhaustible creativity. Because every living creature or inanimate object was suitable material for cursing — "symphony," "present," "Magyars" — indeed, it seemed that the real substance and quality of any word could only be measured by its suitability as an expletive. Strangely enough, despite my many urchin exploits, I almost always got straight A's in school, because the things I needed to know I quickly picked up in passing, not because I felt like learning or from any sense of obligation, but because I felt sorry for my teachers and my still-widowed father and wanted to do it for their sake. At the age of five, then, I was already reading the satiric *Fliegende Blätter* magazine, comparing my vague understanding of family life with the contents of the joke sections: "Oh, those women!" or "Oh, those men!" or "Oh, those mothers-in-law!" When I was six, I beat my father at chess, at seven I wrote a prize-winning essay about the visit of Archduke Franz Karl in Olmütz, and at the age of eight I helped my father do the books for the Bohemian local rail lines under his administration: Kolín–Čerčany and Heřmanův Městec–Borohrádek. And yet the fact remains that I was still an incorrigible street urchin with a mineral collection in one of his pants pocket, a zoo of rain frogs and cockchafers in the other, with blank cartridges and squirt guns at the ready, a cruel mockery of the principles and experiences of educators, the kind of boy Plato would have crowned with a garland of wool and sent to another city as fast as humanly possible; the highest mark of respect that adults could expect from him was a bland, understanding smile.

I was a specialist for markets, where there was always a lot to see and a lot was going on. In Old Town there was the flea market with its narrow stalls full of fabric scraps in every color and pattern and the most mind-boggling junk, used and new, from defunct households or bankrupt stores, vendors and buyers full of suspicion and disdainful hostility, talking big to each other like the heroes of the *Iliad* before the decisive duel. Nearby was Kohlmarkt, where they sold neither cabbage nor coal but mostly just flowers, nothing too fancy, just the soulful flowers of Bohemian country gardens: mignonettes and cockscombs, gillyflowers and wallflowers, geraniums and asters. The market women officiated there in the shadow of the Three Lions Inn, where Mozart once lived. From there it was just a five-minute walk to the Estates Theater, where the orchestra musicians were nervously waiting, as the overture of *The Rake Punished, or Don Giovanni* had not yet even been put to paper and they would have to sight-read when the score was finished, its ink barely dry. The theater, for its part, along with the Karolinum of Charles University — founded by Charles IV, a small man who did great things — overlooked Obstmarkt with its baskets of fruits and berries, resplendent with the bounty of Bohemia's meadows and groves and redolent with the scent of Bohemian forests. But the finest market by far was the

Christmas market on Old Town Square when the booths went up during Advent and were soon covered with snow, because back then it snowed in December in Prague (later, when during the First Republic they moved the market to dreary Karlsplatz, Winter was offended and only sent the bare minimum of snow sometime in January or February). In the jumble of Christmas booths on Old Town Square I sometimes got lost as a child. But I was the only one who noticed, because no on paid any attention to me. By chance I ended back up with my father and his walking companion. There was so much to see. The Bulgarian Duko Petkovich stood there selling Turkish delight, which he cut into portions from a big block using a little hatchet. (Said Willy Haas to Franz Werfel: "I'll give you a florin if you can rhyme something with Duko Petkovich.") And then there was the puppet theater with the sons of kings and enchanted princesses and of course the requisite Faust, to whom a terrifying voice called out in Czech from father Hermann Kafka's haberdashery:

Faust, oh dear Faust, what on earth were you thinking,
sold your soul to the devil without even blinking?!

The miracle of Christmas was multiplied in the booths selling colorful, hand-carved nativity figurines from the Ore Mountains. Dozens of Marys, Josephs, and angels, and hundreds of shepherds and sheep stood lined up in long rows. Snowflakes swirled around Týn Church and the Town Hall, adorning Our Lady of Victory at White Mountain, who dreamily contemplated it all from high atop her column; they caressed the Venus with her mocking smile over on the palace portal, who held an Earth globe between her thighs and, pointing to her loins with her index finder, spoke the frivolous words (in German no less) on a banderole in full public view: "Around this point the whole world turns."

In other words, there were all sorts of homey things, or so it would seem, at least on the thin surface of things or in the peculiar world of a young boy. And yet for all that the nations, denominations and classes were always battle-ready. German fraternity students wearing their colors did not stroll along the Graben for the fun of it, to get some fresh air or to look at the girls, but to show their colors, and the Czech students, who weren't about to be outdone, expressed their convictions with Slavic velvet berets. On Old Town Square, opposite the Habsburg Marian column, they had erected a huge bronze monument to Jan Hus to show that they hadn't forgotten the twenty-seven Protestant Bohemians beheaded by imperial executioners after the Battle of White Mountain. A thing like that is not forgotten. Hus stood there and said — as attested to by the inscription on the pedestal — "Love one another, and let everyone speak his truth," but what he meant was apparently something different: "Just wait until my time comes! I'll show you!" His time, or, rather, the time of those who considered themselves his followers, would come indeed, and once again heads would roll. But still a thing like that is not forgotten. Every house, every street, every square in Prague kept crying out down through the ages: "Don't forget this! Don't forget that!" so that people forgot to live in the present in the face of so much memory and with such a desire for revenge.

This was certainly true of adults. Children may have sometimes been exempt from this. But being grown-up meant remembering, getting even, sometimes with the Germans, sometimes with the Czechs; the Jews were pushed around either way; the aristocrats lived in their own hereafter in Lesser Town, "lesser" meaning "elevated" to a higher power. The boy, who was still indifferent to all of that, slipped through the streets like an eel; played with horse beans on the cobblestones of Teyngässchen; made sure he stayed on good terms with the pickle women on Melantrichgasse, who refreshed him with the cool, sweet and sour juice from their barrels; made friends with a Czech boy in the arcaded courtyard of the House at the Golden Tree on Langengasse, sneaking with him through the maze of houses behind the St. Agnes Cloister and down to the Moldau, which offered all kinds of diversions and flotsam; or played hide-and-seek in the abandoned stairwell of Pachta Palace, which had once belonged to a pleasure-loving countess who was well acquainted with Mozart and Goethe. The boy had a lot to do and think about, the duties of a street urchin are never-ending, and when finally in the evening, much too late, he came running with his tongue hanging out of his mouth, to a dinner table that had already been cleared, he knew his first course would be a few slaps in the face. This bothered him less than being embarrassed by a superfluous caress, because, given that he undertook his longer excursions on laundry days, the main course was bound to be dumplings with white dill sauce anyway.

Once or twice a week the boy's father took him along on

tours of churches and taverns. At Bigalsky's behind St. Henry Church the beer was served in gleaming tankards, hoisted from the cellar through a trapdoor. At Schnell's, in Lesser Town, you drank Pilsner and ate thin, foot-long sausages that were particularly appreciated by the canons from St. Vitus and were therefore known as "canon sausages." But the boy could only enjoy them when his father had his shoes fitted, or tried them on, or picked them up from the shoemaker Chleborád on little Waldsteinplatz. Chleborád's shoes were always too tight but extremely durable. Before entering his shop you fortified yourself at Schnell's, and afterwards you went to rest in the shade of St. Nicholas Church at Glaubitz's, where King Wenceslaus IV himself had been fond of boozing it up. The way home was then long enough to decide if you would make another stop at the "Infant Jesus" or at the Pinkas tavern nearby Our Lady of the Snows. In Prague there was often something sacred involved. If it was warm, the preferred destination was the shady brewery garden of St. Thomas Monastery or the Primates' tavern, emblazoned with the inscription:

June, July and August the heat is hellish:
Forget about the wife and drink with relish,

or you went to Fleck's or to the "Black Brewery." There were other beer gardens too, and the boy knew them all, was personally acquainted with the radish women or the ones peddling candied almonds, or the ones with rollmops, peppered fish and pickled onions in their shoulder baskets, not to mention the men balancing trays on their head with candied fruit arrayed on sticks, the lottery men, the love-meter men, Ferda Springauf, the man with the electrostatic generator, the balloon vendor, the retired scribe who demonstrated roly-poly dolls and wind-up walruses — in short, a great big merry traveling fair which did its rounds from one beer garden to the next.

It was a peaceful, agreeable atmosphere until some animated group would begin to sing at their table, not really for the sake of singing but in order to make a point:

It lives, it lives, the Slavic spirit,
defiantly it flowers.
With us is Russia! Our attackers
the Frenchman overpowers!

This was forbidden, of course, by Imperial and Royal decree. But some Germans at the neighboring table had supposedly started to sing "The Watch on the Rhine," a tune that was likewise prohibited. Russia was far away, as were France and the Rhine. And the Germans had actually sung "The Lorelei," but the Czechs maintained it had been "The Watch on the Rhine," and anyway someone had loudly and clearly referred to the town of Aussig as Aussig and not Ústí, as the Slavic spirit necessitated. And so the peaceful atmosphere went up in smoke and the age-old grudge, borne since the days of the Přemyslids, the Luxembourgers and the Decree of Kutná Hora, was vented in a brawling, brutal, beer-glass-smashing fashion.

The most outlandish private destinies became linked, over time, to national passions. And one of the most bizarre was related to me by my father when once again we were in St. Vitus Cathedral visiting the burial chapel of Saint Wenceslaus, the first Duke of Bohemia and patron saint of the Czechs, who was stabbed to death on his way to mass by his cruel and Germanophobic brother Boleslaus. Almost a millennium had passed since then, but the Czechs had been singing their poignant song for almost just as long:

Saint Wenceslaus, Duke of the Bohemian Land,
suffer not us nor our children to perish.

The door ring the collapsing prince had tried to hold on to can still be seen at the entrance of the chapel, and the chapel itself, henceforth a mausoleum to the saint, was completely bedecked with carnelians and agates, with amethysts and chrysoprases, as found in abundance in the magic mountains of Bohemia. It was not, however, the medieval pomp and splendor of the chamber and not the fate of the princely martyr that appealed to me the most, but an iron door off in the corner, sealed with seven locks, whose keys were in the custody of the seven highest dignitaries of the Crown, the Church, and the Capital. My father could list them all by rank and name: the governor, the cardinal, the chief provincial marshal, the chief burgrave, the chief justice of the supreme court, the corps commander, and the burgomaster. Only when all seven keys were together could this door be opened. It led to the vault of the Bohemian Crown Jewels, where the crown, scepter and imperial orb of the "Father of the Fatherland," Charles IV, where regalia, insignia and other precious objects have been kept for more than six centuries.

All of that had been described many times before. What was not known to the public, what has never been written about and what I am making known here for the first time, is the story of Virgil Suchý, chief clerk of the provincial chancellery, who had succeeded in making the seemingly impossible possible, that is to say, getting hold of all seven keys and entering the Crown Vault at night. He paid for this foolhardy deed with his life. But it wasn't as if he had wanted to rob the vault. Rather, Virgil Suchý was an ardent Czech patriot, the kind who passionately demanded the crowning of Franz Joseph as King of Bohemia as *unum necessarium*, the kind who was imbued with the legendary, nay, mythical power of those jewels in which the grandeur of Bohemia found its expression and who in his bachelor's existence was inspired, indeed possessed, by nothing else but the desire to see and touch these magic symbols.

Given that he was an acquaintance of my father, my father having tutored him in German in his student days so that he could apply for a public administration position, my father was sufficiently informed about Chief Clerk of the Provincial Chancellery Suchý, his daring enterprise and its outcome. The authorities themselves had of course kept a lid on the whole affair, which indeed was rather embarrassing. For the fact that a mid-level public official should have succeeded in prying the famed seven keys from the hands of the highest dignitaries was indeed tantamount to a sevenfold dereliction of duty and was an example of that grandiose, sometimes endearing, sometimes creative slovenliness that, as people occasionally jested, was the glue that held the dual monarchy together but which ultimately spelled its doom.

How the chief clerk of the provincial chancellery managed to get hold of all seven keys perhaps belongs in the realm of

Magical Physics, whose theory of a persistent concentration of the greatest force in the smallest possible area promises ultimate victory over even the most insurmountable obstacles. Had the confirmed bachelor Virgil Suchý, instead of concentrating his efforts on the seven keys, used the same manic persistence to look for, say, the cancer bacillus or a way to square the circle with a straightedge and compass, he would have, said my father, inevitably won the Nobel Prize. And yet he considered it his mission in life to attain the seven keys. Using all manner of clever pretenses, conclusive reports about the necessity of structural repairs, the need for intermittent cleaning, for a more dependable and dignified storage of the treasures, for controlling the temperature and relative humidity of the glass display cases, for the scientific indispensability of historically significant measurements, for an exact inventory of the jewels as well as the caratage of the gold, and whatever else an exact and realistic imagination might come up with in terms of valid and seemingly legal reasons for the unnecessary and the unauthorized, Suchý succeeded in convincing his superiors and his superiors' superiors, including the Cabinet Chancellery in Vienna, of the urgent need to inspect the crown treasury, and prudently had these individual actions converge in such a way that ultimately the seven keys found their way into the safe of the chief provincial marshal on the day before he planned to open the door. Although all seven dignitaries were supposed to attend this rather important official act in person, the president of the provincial court was laid up in bed with a sore throat, the corps commander was away on an inspection tour, the chief burgrave had traveled to Styria for the wedding of his eldest son, and, in general, after much back and forth, everyone had taken the whole thing lightly, as is the tendency of Austrians, and so the keys had been deposited with the chief provincial marshal, which the scrupulously shrewd Suchý had evidently counted on. Incidentally, the planned technical inspections and measures were expected to take several days, and so it was impossible for the highest authorities themselves to monitor around the clock who went in and out of the vault. This was the task, when the time came, of the civilian supervisory bodies appointed by the governor together with the military sentries provided by the corps commander. But one relied on the other, the supervisory system was not yet fully regulated, questions of this sort needed to be settled through official channels, whose barriers and hurdles the chief clerk of the provincial chancellery skillfully knew how to multiply. The safe with the keys, however, was located in the antechamber of the chief provincial marshal. And this just so happened to be the room where Suchý worked, who was the only one besides his boss who knew the — in those days rather primitive — combination of the lock. On this fateful day, the combined power of the seven Crown keys having thus been placed in Suchý's heinous hands, the latter went to the cathedral after work, took part in the litany and blessing, and then allowed himself to be locked in the giant Gothic hall unnoticed, with its many nooks and crannies, altars, sarcophagi, kneelers and monuments. Up to this point, Suchý's actions can be reconstructed with considerable precision. Our knowledge of what he did after that is fragmentary at best; the authorities tried to cover it up or deny it, pass it off as a legend, but in a country so rife with conflict and contradiction, only common knowledge is sometimes treated as confidential and secret, whereas the things that are truly secret generally come to light with bared teeth.

When on the following morning the distinguished gentlemen were supposed to gather at the Saint Wenceslaus Chapel, only three of the dignitaries showed up at first. Three had excused themselves, and the chief provincial marshal, arriving very late and in quite a tizzy, informed the others that his safe had been opened, that the seven keys were gone, and that Chief Clerk of the Provincial Chancellery Virgil Suchý was nowhere to be found.

"You can imagine," my father said, "the sheepish faces of the cardinal and governor upon hearing this, as well as the likely gloating face of the burgomaster, who couldn't stand the chief provincial marshal. All three had yet to take a closer look at the iron door to the vault, which seemed locked as always, and the governor had used the time they spent waiting to gripe about the corps commander for failing to post any sentries. He wisely remained silent about his own responsibility to designate the appropriate civilian supervisory bodies. Upon hearing the shocking news from the chief provincial marshal they now all ran to the corner with the iron door and found that, far from being locked as they'd assumed, it had actually been left ajar.

"With a horror that gripped even the burgomaster, the four gentlemen filed up the ancient, dark spiral staircase leading to the treasury, cold sweat on their brows, limbs shaking, pulses beating irregularly. The vision of the seemingly inevitable theft of the Imperial Crown Jewels filled them not only with a principled and patriotic loathing but also with personal anxiety. The cardinal and the burgomaster had the least to fear. No one could depose them. But the governor and the chief provincial marshal could expect the worst, and saw themselves being struck down by imperial thunderbolts; the scandal would take on global proportions, they would become laughingstocks, and clearing their names would be an infernally difficult task if wagging tongues took an admittedly inexcusable dereliction of duty and framed it as a treasonous political crime. The one-floor climb up the spiral staircase seemed interminably long to them, and since the obese and panting chief provincial marshal was leading the way at a crawling pace, he being the most severely affected and hence bent with misery, the steep and narrow ascent was much slower and torturous than the trim and elegant cardinal would have wished, who indeed, as a former calvary officer, would have reached his destination with a couple of vigorous leaps and bounds if left to his own devices. The governor, too, whom the people referred to as 'long Franzl' because of his tall stature, could hardly contain his impatience, while the burgomaster seemed content to bring up the rear, suffering as he did from vertigo.

"But the astonishing sight awaiting the four dignitaries in the Crown Vault would present itself to them soon enough. On the only piece of furniture in the room, an old throne with faded wine-red velvet upholstery, sat slumped the figure of the chief clerk of the provincial chancellery, Virgil Suchý, attired in the dalmatics of the Bohemian kings, the crown of Charles IV on his head, and the scepter in his clenched right hand, while the imperial orb in the other had apparently been dropped and rolled off into a corner of the room. That Suchý was dead was indisputable, his vacant eyes stared blankly at the imperial orb, which must have been the last thing his dying gaze beheld, his tongue sticking out at the dignitaries in one last derisive gesture, while a final, eerie laugh had frozen on his twisted face. And no wonder, for his situation was singular enough to be so tragic that it suddenly killed him, and comical enough that when his final thought crossed his mind that he, Chief Clerk of the Provincial Chancellery Virgil Suchý, was the last crowned Czech, he broke into a fanatical laughter that distorted his face for good. It seemed as if this laughter was still echoing in the room, indeed perhaps this grotesque laughter had shattered the glass display cases when Suchý entered the vault and then, while he was dressing, only grew more piercing. But below the royal regalia, hanging down to the floor, were Suchý's short legs in gray-and-black striped pants with yellow lace-up shoes. 'He's dead,' said the chief provincial marshal. 'Nothing seems to be missing,' declared the governor. 'The display cases can be repaired,' noted the burgomaster. 'We'd better not mention this to anyone,' advised the cardinal."

"How do you know what the gentlemen said?" I asked my father.

"Always too curious for your own good, aren't you. People just know these kinds of things. What else were they supposed to say? In any case, this incredible story was withheld from the general public, and if anyone dared allude to it they risked their job, if not worse. Because no one could ever prove the incident even happened. What can be proven at all? And by whom? It's easy to say that Suchý had been crazy from the start. How many people who've done the most adventurous and superfluous things has the world considered perfectly normal and held in the highest esteem? Of course it's entirely possible that Virgil Suchý was not merely driven by patriotic fervor, but by a fascination with the mystical number seven and that, had there only been a single lock, his interest would have faded. Maybe it was just a strange coincidence that right when he was putting on the jewels he suffered a long overdue apoplexy. But maybe — and I consider this the most plausible explanation — the jewels possess a secret power that lends strength to their rightful bearer and destroys anyone who usurps them. Because this is what people say, and has even been given as a reason why the Habsburgs were never as lucky as the kings of Bohemia or never even had themselves crowned in the first place."

The story of Virgil Suchý and the Bohemian Crown Jewels was just one of the many abstruse secret legends linked to almost every location in Prague, a bewildering tapestry of myth and lore zealously woven by every nation, religion and class. Yet there was a common thread, from which the ambiguous, skillfully interwoven fabric unfolded with all of its incomparable and unforgettable runic characters. One of these runes is the much-maligned Prague German, the High German of the Imperial Chancellery of Charles IV, which its great chancellor, John of Neumarkt, elevated into a written language, free of dialect, neatly polished and incorruptible as a diamond, the German of *The Sonnets to Orpheus*, of *The Trial* and *The Castle*, of *The Friend of the World* and *One Another*, of *Tycho Brahe* and *Reubeni*, outlasting in these last poetic monuments the dubiousness of the era. Otherwise the German runes of Prague have all been torn asunder, for they were never really appreciated, neither by the Czechs nor by the other Germans, including the ones in Bohemia, indeed were scarcely perceived, and were hence destroyed by all and sundry. And so the Czechs in Prague are finally alone, just like they always wanted to be.

The boy and subsequent man was destined, or condemned, to look back from other cities at the relief of old Prague. When, years ago, he first walked down Broadway, the swaying of the ocean liner still in his limbs, the skyscrapers ominously breathing down his neck, he heard two old women talking in Czech. He approached them with the eagerness of a stranger gripped by a long-lost sound. For two generations they had lived in the vast and boisterous city of New York, even their sons were dyed-in the-wool Americans. "And you," they asked me, "where are you from?" — "I'm a German from Prague." — "Oh, from Prague," they marveled, "so you're from the big city."

The big, the great is what has passed through eras of unimaginable duration, through passions, the desire to live and create, and what has been inherited through the struggles and turmoil of the ages. Greatness is the fruit of longing, the Athens of yore, the Rome of yore, the Prague of yore, a city of ruins even if its houses and magnificent buildings remain intact. Great is what remains in the spirit of the heart.

LEFT PANEL

The Wellner Case

In my younger days I once made the acquaintance of a certain Jakob Wellner, who for years invested all his energy, and eventually all of his financial resources, in an unusual litigation against City Hall. The Wellner case against the Municipality of Prague was notable to me not just for its legal peculiarity, but especially for its psychological aspects. To this day I'm still in possession of some notes pertaining to these legal matters and certain related events, for the case deeply affected my own life as well.

It began for me as a student when, each day for a little while, I was entrusted with the task of looking after the son of Jakob Wellner and his wife Carola. The son's name was Helmuth.

Jakob Wellner was the last or, counting Helmuth, the next-to-last scion of an old Prague burgher family of considerable means. Carola Wellner (née Kaltenbrunn) was likewise the last in a line of lesser Bohemian nobility whose name was mentioned among those loyal to the emperor during the turmoil of the Thirty Years' War. She was delicate and tranquil of nature, was always friendly and never in a rush, which, although she was anything but a beauty, gave her a pleasing amiability in her middle years. Her husband, when I first met him, was on the wrong side of fifty.

Having sufficient means at his disposal, he had withdrawn from the world of business and, in lieu of anything else to do, though more so from a deep-seated inner impulse, devoted himself to the study of genealogy. Not only did he possess bundle upon bundle of ancient family documents but he constantly added to them from church records, land registers, as well as from official and private archives, not just in Prague but all over the country and abroad, wherever a family member had lived or sojourned, copying out everything of even the remotest interest to the Wellners. Just as other well-off individuals collect paintings, prints, glassware or coins, transforming these into their own personal kingdoms which they subsequently govern, arrange and expand, fancying these collections as a reflection of themselves, in their own eyes and in the eyes of others, so it was that Wellner collected documents relating to his family history, piling them up in neatly labeled folders which he kept on special shelves, recording them in registers, charts and family trees, discovering in the process ever new connections between individuals and family lines, and busying himself, so to speak, almost exclusively with his own self-discovery by means of tracing and verifying these lines that, rescued from the obscurity of history, converged from all sides in himself.

His wife Carola might have seen this pursuit as rooted in his need for distraction from the tribulations caused by their son, Helmuth. Helmuth was sixteen years old, three years younger than me, when, answering an ad in the paper, I assumed more the role of his companion rather than his tutor. It soon became clear to me that Helmuth's difficulties finding his way in life could be put down to his permanent state of suspicion, expressed in his behavior as alternating modes of defense and attack. His movements were abrupt, erratic and expansive; his speech came in clumps of words, rarely in complete sentences, and was often shot through with inexplicable questions. A sudden "How come?" uttered completely out of context and unexpectedly continuing a hidden thought out loud was among his most frequent forms of expression.

I had taken it upon myself to discover the source of this malady and perhaps, by addressing its root cause, to help him overcome it; and so the antiquarian preoccupations of Herr Wellner were not unwelcome to me at first, as I hoped that they might shed some light on certain hereditary predispositions. I took my new job very seriously. I studied a significant number of works of medical psychology and the physiology of the senses, from the oldest to the then newest, the nascent Viennese School still struggling for recognition. But the main purpose of my dealings with Helmuth, the way I saw it, had always been to win his trust through a maximum of sympathy and understanding; indeed, this seemed to me (and still does today) to be the best and most reliable therapy one person can offer another.

Not that young Helmuth had met with a lack of love from his parents; he was an only child, after all, with a radiant name to boot, literally meaning "hale of spirit." But this love, and the best will of his parents to show it, was progressively overshadowed by the counterpoint of disappointment caused by the fact that this son, from early childhood, had resisted the normal course of education, failed to satisfy the requirements of any subject matter or, rather, strayed before long into other matters, was unable to win any playmates, indeed didn't even induce that sense of rivalry in others that is otherwise one of the most important sources of development in one's boyhood years. They had to take him out of elementary school after several failed attempts and entrust him instead to private tutors, each of whom had soon given up as hopeless their efforts to discipline and systematically educate the child.

I was now the latest, and Frau Wellner had taken me on with the express wish: "Don't give him lessons like a schoolmaster, it's pointless. Perhaps you'll succeed in becoming his friend and companion." That was an uncommonly sensible remark for a bourgeois mother to make, and I answered her by saying: "Maybe he'll give *me* lessons and become *my* friend and companion."

I made sure not to put him under any kind of pressure during our first meeting, having resolved to be as receptive as possible. We went for a walk through Old Town, without exchanging a word at first. It was early autumn, that cozy time of year with its limpid afternoon light that lends the crests and cornices of buildings a fine, golden contour and when the bustle in the streets heralds a vigorous new beginning after the summer break. Helmuth walked beside me, now and then casting a probing glance at me, as if he were carefully sounding out what he could expect from me. He was a good head taller than me, with a powerful, bulky build and limbs, and his light-blue eyes had a certain flicker, always searching and ceaselessly busy. Only after some time did he begin to speak. "I much prefer alone. Walk the streets for myself." But it was my task to accompany him, if only because Helmuth, when left to his own devices, would inevitably get embroiled in conflict with pedestrians or shopkeepers, beginning to quarrel for whatever reason and putting them in their place, possibly not without good reason but which nonetheless caused difficulties — an embarrassment for his parents, and sometimes costly. Once, for example, he had taken a bunch of dill pickles from an open barrel outside a grocery store and handed them out to a swarm of boys who scattered when the grocer came out and demanded that Helmuth pay for them, whereas Helmuth, in turn, pointed out to the grocer that the pickles by rights belonged to the boys since they knew how to appreciate them. He couldn't, in other words, be left to roam the streets on his own. "I also prefer to take walks on my own," I said, "but I can't do everything the way I want."

"Mama says you my friend. You my friend? How come? Father paying."

To deny I was being paid would have been foolish and, what's more, untrue. So I said, "Look, Helmuth, I'm poor and have to earn some money somehow. I thought you might be able to help me a little by putting up with my company. That would truly be a good and noble deed. But if you don't want to then I guess I'll have to pack it in, and will probably spend a long time trying to find some other source of income."

"Pack it in? How come?" he said, alarmed. "No, no, don't pack. You poor? How come? I give you money. Here. Five crowns."

"Thank you. Five crowns? That's a lot! I could use it to buy a book I've been wanting. But, no, I can't accept it."

"Why not accept it?" he shouted. "Take! Which book?"

Obviously I had no intention of letting him buy me a book. But I resorted to this white lie so he would take an interest in me and to give him the feeling I was dependent on him and not the other way around, that he had something to offer me in this, our new relationship. We were standing outside Calve's, the old bookshop on Kleiner Ring in Old Town.

"Which book," he cried, "which one?"

I couldn't think of much on the spur of the moment, so I just said: "I wanted, uh . . . *The New Life* by Dante, an Italian poet."

"I'll buy," shouted Helmuth enthusiastically, charging into the store. "Quick, *The New Life*," he said to the shop clerk, "by Italian poet."

"Yes, of course, by Dante," answered the clerk.

"Make it snappy," said Helmuth, "bring now. Why wait?"

"I'll fetch it from the storeroom immediately," said the clerk, "but which translation? Which edition? Or would you like to have it in Italian?"

Helmuth looked at me, at a loss.

"Oh, just the translation published by Reclam," I said.

It was a stapled paperback edition for less than two crowns.

"So cheap," said a crestfallen Helmuth. "But I have five crowns."

"It'll certainly do," I said, "and I thank you from the bottom of my heart, Helmuth."

"How come?" he cried cheerfully, "Don't mention it. Can I read too? With you? Oh, what a wonderful walk!"

It was perhaps not the most felicitous idea to tell him that this was the book I wanted, since I'd now have to discuss it with Helmuth, a work leading straight into the thorny realm of Eros, which no doubt intensely preoccupied the mind of a sixteen-year-old but could surely not be interpreted by a nineteen-year-old with any degree of self-assurance. I was also afraid that Frau Carola and, even more so, her husband might object to this choice of reading material. I immediately told his mother about it the following afternoon, what had happened, what my underlying intention had been, and that regrettably, at that particular moment, it was the only book that had come to mind. To my surprise, she was greatly pleased about what had happened, even adamantly refusing to let me reimburse her.

"Don't worry about it," she said. "Helmuth told us all about it yesterday. He was in a remarkably good mood, extremely approachable." And so in the days that followed the two of us read Dante's confessions together, and I tried to explain it to him to the extent that I myself understood, especially about how love could turn you into a poet, and that, by the same token, it was the poet more than anyone who understood how to love with particular depth and truthfulness and was capable, by virtue of his art form, of immortalizing his feelings. I considered myself an expert in this, for I had my first heartaches and hence my first poems behind me, which had even appeared in a Berlin literary journal of some repute. Helmuth listened raptly to everything I said, asked an enormous number of questions, many of which were hard to answer; but it hardly fazed him when I told him straight out that I didn't yet know about this or that. Indeed, he seemed in these moments to feel a particular kinship with me.

In a mere few weeks we had developed an auspicious rapport. I had also brought him to my room once, revealing to him the little world I'd built for myself in my father's apartment: the books; the Japanese woodcut pinned to the wall that depicted an actor in the role of a sword-wielding samurai whose blue and yellow kimono stood out against a vast seascape and a sun-drenched, glowing firmament, above which a ghostly flock of black birds boded sinister things to come; my mineral collection; but above all my manuscripts containing poems and my attempts at prose. Helmuth marveled at all of this, wished he had the same, and even began to write his own poetry, which I welcomed wholeheartedly, as it seemed to help him to collect and order his feelings and thoughts; it bound him to certain rhythms, gave us the opportunity to talk about certain things, and was a gratifying achievement in its own right. Poetry as a therapeutic method is not a new discovery, indeed its very healing power is possibly one of its prime causes. His attempts to write poetry brought me closer to Helmuth, and to this day I still have a few of his peculiar poems. These and a couple of notes constitute the few tangible mementos of our curious companionship.

Pavement and patterns
of blue and white stone.
I only step on blue,

on white I feel alone.
Lone girl
here in the alley
comes on white stones
not to me.

Herr Wellner called me into his study one afternoon. On his desk were giant piles of paper, documents, books and fascicles pedantically ordered and behind which he was nearly hidden from view.

"Could you spare a little more time than usual?" he asked peeping out from his paperwork. "I don't mean for Helmuth. I'm quite satisfied with his progress. But perhaps you could set aside another two hours or so a day for something else I have in mind which I'll gladly make worth your while. I'm referring to some confidential copying work I'd like to have done here in my apartment."

I said that, in principle, I'd be happy to do that kind of work. I was at the very beginning of my university studies, and it was at least another year or more until my first exams. I usually only attended lectures in the morning or evening anyway.

"It concerns the documents of a legal case," Herr Wellner explained, "a great variety of documents, I should add, excerpts from books, transcripts of all kinds of records, from the fifteenth century down to the present. I have a typewriter here. I would need five copies of each of the specified documents."

I openly admitted that I wasn't very nimble on a typewriter, that I could actually only hunt and peck with my right finger and that I was wholly deficient in the wonderful art of typing with both hands at once (which is still the case today, by the way).

"You'll manage just fine," Herr Wellner reassured me. "You'll get the hang of it; and it's nothing urgent. The main thing is I can count on your discretion."

"Yes, you certainly can. But what will I say if Helmuth asks me what I'm doing here in your study? It wouldn't be good for our relationship, now that we're on such good terms, if suddenly I was keeping secrets from him, and with his father at that. I'm afraid he wouldn't handle it well."

"That may well be. And yet still I'd prefer not to tell him what it's about. He would go and tell everyone, and that would be the worst thing that could happen in such a delicate matter."

"Would it not be possible to include him somehow, to make him my collaborator, so that he has the feeling he's helping out with an important and useful task and has a shared responsibility? Then we could count on his discretion, I think. Excluding him entirely seems wrong to me. In that case you'd be better off hiring someone else, although even then it wouldn't be easy, and probably not very wise, to keep Helmuth away from someone who is working in your home on a daily basis."

Herr Wellner pondered this for a while. "Maybe you're right," he said. "He shouldn't get the feeling that there's some kind of conspiracy going on, which he'd surely think has something to do with him. Try to cautiously get him involved in your work. It'll be your job to keep him quiet. You'll surely do better than me."

The matter at hand was indeed as strange as it was in need of discretion. A long time ago, Herr Wellner had found among his family documents an ancient legal title of considerable import dating back to the reign of Wenceslaus IV, King of Bohemia and son of Emperor Charles IV. One of his ancestors at that time had been granted the right to ferry passengers at the very spot on the Moldau where the Emperor Franz I Bridge would later be erected. When eventually the bridge was built, no one thought anymore about these long since forgotten but by no means abolished or compensated ferrying rights. Herr Wellner's father, who had never concerned himself with genealogy and never studied the respective documents, indeed probably didn't even have or know about them, had shown no interest in the construction of the bridge. But the fact that he raised no objection did nothing to alter the continued existence of the family's ferrying rights, the transference of which was documented and expressly linked to the clause that the Wellner family, and only the Wellner family, was granted by the king for all time the right to provide communication between each bank of the Moldau at this particular spot, that said right should never and in no form be encroached upon, modified, or abolished by similar rights, concessions, structures or measures save through the voluntary abdication or sale of these rights by their owner. *Datum et manu propria Nostra sigilloque Nostro confirmatum in castello Nostro Karlstejnensi Die Quinta Mensis Maii Anno Domini 1405* — "Given with Our own hand and confirmed with Our seal at Our Karlštejn Castle this 5th of May 1405."

These ferrying rights were subsequently exercised by the family for several generations until one of the Wellners turned to a different pursuit and let others do the ferrying, without, however, expressly ceding the respective rights to them. Rather, these rights by law remained with the family until finally none of the family members paid heed to them any longer, so that in the course of time virtually no one even knew anything about them. Other ferries and crossing points had meanwhile started operating. And little by little the Wellners made their fortune by other means. So when the bridge was built, it didn't occur to anyone that there was any such established and inalienable right that needed to be taken into account. Herr Wellner now intended to assert this right, in conflict as it was with the subsequent right of custom arising from the longstanding use of the bridge, while at the same time making a hefty compensation claim. The bridge, in his view, had at any rate been wrongfully built, and he planned to back up his claims with all the materials at his disposal; once the latter had been duly gathered, he would hire the best lawyers, whatever the cost, to make his case unassailable.

"Where would we end up," he said, "if a vested right could simply be nullified arbitrarily. Even a municipality can't just take what it thinks it needs. It would spell the end of our civilization if we start to make distinctions between private and social morality. And don't go thinking I'm in it for the money; the money is just to substantiate the claim. What I'm concerned about is the essence of the law, which I want to establish unambiguously."

Why it was the Wellner family that was awarded these ferrying rights is explained by a document I was supposed to transcribe, a letter from a knight, Baworek von Schwamberg, to the abbot of Teplá Abbey. Herr Wellner, whose efforts over the years had turned him into a specialist in old manuscripts, was in possession of this document and had deciphered the old German script that was almost illegible to an untrained eye. The text, which I jotted down for myself as well, was sensational enough:

"The life of our gracious lord of Bohemia was spared through the aid of God from coming to an abrupt end. The king, on this second day of Easter, had been carousing with friends under Vyssegrad. During which carousing, he tried to have his way with the young wife of Perchtold, the burgrave, having dispatched the burgrave to deliver some letters so as to be alone with her. But the latter forthwith caught the king in bed with his wife and threatened to kill him in the heat of the moment. The lord, in his shirtsleeves, sprang to his feet and into his saddle, heading towards the Moldau, but the impetuous burgrave pursued him in his fury. Yet the king reached the boat of a ferryman who brought him safely to the other side, for which the lord wished to recompense him, bestowing on the ferryman and his kin a perpetual reward in that henceforth he alone, and no one else, with skiff, punt, or bridge, have such right of transport at that spot of the river."

This letter from the year 1405 corroborated unmistakably the official transfer of the privilege while shedding light on the character of a Bohemian monarch who, though not entirely devoid of talent, went down in history with the moniker "the Idle," having time and again fallen prey to his passions.

Whether the man who brought the king to safety on the opposite bank of the river was really called Wellner, "wave-maker," or was simply being referred to as such on account of his occupation on the waves of the Moldau is unclear. It appeared, at any rate, to be a demonstrable fact that one of his descendants, likewise called Wellner, was operating a ferry at the same spot two centuries later during the Thirty Years' War. For a tombstone set in the floor of Prague's venerable Church of Our Lady of the Snows contains the following inscription in faulty Latin:

DOMINUS
CHRISTOPHORUS UNDUARIUS
REGIA GRATIA MULTAVIAE FLUMINIS RIPARUM
CONECTOR ET PORTITOR
CIVIS PRAGENSIS
OBIIT DIE X MENSIS APRILIS A. D. MDCXXX

indicating that said Unduarius, a.k.a. Wellner, who died on April 10, 1630, and incidentally bore the very fitting name of Christopher, the saint who carried the Christ child across a river, must have enjoyed a considerable reputation, being referred to explicitly as *dominus*, and citizen or burgher of Prague, while his function as "connector of the river banks" is commemorated with a certain pomp. His royal privilege is also emphasized. The marble tombstone alone testifies to the fact that he was a respected and propertied man.

The Wellners, though, had documents from as recent as the

late eighteenth century showing the family's continual ownership of the land where the two heads of the subsequent bridge would be built, with repeated reference being made to the ferry operated there by the family, even though in later years this was presumably only a minor source of income for them, who were variously referred to in Prague chronicles as the owners of different buildings as well as being guild masters of the tanners, saddlers and even the brewers. Of particular importance, moreover, was an official document from 1790 issued by the municipal government of Prague and attesting to an agreement reached between the City and one Anton Christoph Wellner, in which he "agrees to convey, free of charge and as urgency requires, aldermen, watchmen and members of the court on his inherited family-owned Moldau ferry north of Shooters Island in exchange for the concession of one acre of municipal land at the upper end of the Horse Market for the purpose of erecting a brewery." And, indeed, one of the breweries at the upper end of what used to be the Horse Market (latterly known as Wenceslas Square) was still owned by the Wellners in the mid-eighteenth century.

Subsequent documents attested to a certain confusion, as the municipality's concession of the brewery property was apparently viewed by some as compensation in lieu of the ferrying rights, whereas in reality it was remuneration for a regular service provided to the city by the Wellners on their "inherited and family-owned" ferry, as the latter was expressly referred to in 1790. The matter became more obscure after that. And this was precisely the point of contention on which Jakob Wellner wished to make his case and from which he sought to argue that the municipality had the obligation to make substantial restitution.

The number of written documents that needed to be copied or excerpted to establish the legal basis of his case ran into the hundreds, as they included not only documentation of the immediate claim, its incontestability and continued existence, but also a vast number of papers proving the order of hereditary succession and supporting the claim by reference to legal precedents and relevant albeit often rather convoluted legal provisions in older and newer Bohemian and Austrian law. There was no telling how extensive this task would be and how long it would take me to do it (especially considering my one-finger typing method). The enormity of this juridical skyscraper, which Herr Wellner had been erecting for years and for which, in the fullness of time, he planned to engage the best legal minds, at any rate held a certain fascination for me.

The first task I gave to Helmuth was to verify the chronological order of certain papers that needed to be transcribed, a rather superfluous task given the fastidiousness of Herr Wellner. I also asked him to dictate the simpler texts to me for typing, which seemed a good exercise for him, though it tended to hinder rather than facilitate my progress. His desire to learn about each document was tremendous. And this was precisely the reason I ran into considerable difficulties on one of the first afternoons. He had read the aforementioned letter by the knight Bahorek von Schwamberg relating the origins of the royal privilege and referring to the king's dubious affair with the wife of Perchtold, the Vyšehrad burgrave.

"How come," he cried, "this king! When he did wrong! Burgrave in the right! Wellner in the wrong. Was rewarded for it. All Wellners in the wrong. What happened to burgrave? And his wife?"

Nothing more was known about the fate of his wife, unlike the Vyšehrad burgrave Perchtold, whose body was dragged from the Moldau downstream from Charles Bridge a few days after the king's miraculous rescue. Whether this was an accident or whether the same dark forces were at work which, some years before, had tortured John of Nepomuk, the vicar general of the Prague archbishopric, at the behest of the king and thrown his body into the river from that very bridge, who really knows? The cleric, at any rate, was canonized, and to this day his bronze statue adorns the venerable Prague bridge, whereas no one ever bothered to commemorate Burgrave Perchtold. I said nothing about this to Helmuth. And that was a mistake.

"The king's injustice," I tried to explain, "is *one* thing. His rescue is *another*. The wrong he did was a personal matter. Wellner, the ferryman, didn't rescue an individual, he saved the monarch, the crowned and anointed head of state."

"How come? King and person, same thing! You only save kings, not people? If the burgrave . . . and instead of the king an ordinary person had offended him, made him a cuckold . . . and the burgrave wanted to kill him: would Wellner not have helped then? And that would have been okay?" It was typical of Helmuth that when he was agitated he spoke much more clearly than usual, his sentences more complete.

"It would not have been okay," I said, "but, yes, it might have happened that way."

"So only because a bad king, a bad person was saved, by this Wellner . . . that's the only reason the Wellners are rich and richer . . . Tower of evil. Every bread roll I eat, bought with evil money . . . We're guilty . . . Should all stand trial!"

"You're forgetting, Helmuth, that it's our duty to rescue a person in distress. Always. A doctor will also heal a wounded wrongdoer."

"Something's rotten," he cried. "Wellner was paid for it."

"But he hadn't been expecting any payment when he rescued the king. He couldn't even know who was right. He received his privilege afterward, without having asked for it."

"He knew it then. How come? Shouldn't have accepted it . . . Should have begged the burgrave for forgiveness . . . Only then a good deed . . . What happened to burgrave?"

"So you're firmly convinced the burgrave was right in wanting to kill the king? You believe that the king's sin was deserving of death? And you believe that each of us has the right to pass judgment and immediately carry out the sentence ourselves?"

Helmuth thought for a while. You could see it cost him a lot of effort. Then he said: "Burgrave maybe too hotheaded . . . Wellner wants to help . . . I get it . . . King was fearful . . . I get it . . . But the whole thing's a terrible injustice," he then said, bursting forth in a complete sentence. "The king should have first atoned, made amends. Did he? And if not, then

Wellner's deed was an injustice and the payment he accepted for it an even greater one."

Our discussion was going nowhere. I was afraid my attempt to involve Helmuth would come to naught. What's more, his uncompromising ideas of right and wrong were threatening to shake the foundations of his relationship to his parents and the world. That my fears were not unfounded became apparent the very next day. Shaking all over, Helmuth approached me, and without even returning my greeting he cried: "Why didn't you tell me about the burgrave? I didn't sleep at all last night . . . The papers . . . I read them. The burgrave was thrown into Moldau, afterward . . . Who did it? . . . Murderous king . . . Our money comes from him."

"There's no proof that King Wenceslaus had a hand in the death of the burgrave. It could have been the hasty deed of some courtier, and the king knew nothing about it. Maybe it was even just an accident, an unfortunate chain of circumstances." Helmuth looked at me for a while. Tears filled his eyes. Then he went to the window and said: "Shame on you."

I bit my lips and was silent. After a long pause, Helmuth turned to me again and said in one fluent sentence: "You know well enough that King Wenceslaus IV had your patron saint and namesake, Saint John, thrown into the Moldau and done away with." This sentence was followed by his usual fragmentary speech, as he blurted out the words: "I leaving this house . . . Becoming gardener's boy . . . Gardener's boy, yes . . . Earn my keep . . ."

I'd meanwhile regained my composure. "Listen, Helmuth,"

I said. "I'm not a judge. Neither of us is a judge. Nobody is, when you get right down to it. In reality the judging is done somewhere else. No one knows where. But it's likely done completely differently than how we think it should be. Otherwise there wouldn't be so many things happening in the world that we don't agree with. You and I both. We're all born 'into' a world that is partly finished and partly still being formed. As a poet you must have noticed that. We can't change the things that are done. We can only contribute to the part that is still in the making."

"Yeah, yeah, yeah . . . How come . . . For that reason . . . Not me with this injustice."

"No one says you should. I'm not much older than you. I know too little. I can't change the whole world after the fact. It seems it's not perfect anywhere. There's a bit of injustice woven into everything. That's the first bitter experience we make. That's our confirmation. I know this much: If you want to live, you have to worm your way through."

This remark of mine was fatal. I noticed it the very moment the words crossed my lips. Helmuth looked up. "Do you *have* to want to live?" he then asked.

That afternoon I explained to Herr Wellner that I did not want to continue with the copying work I'd agreed to. I told him about the effect this family history was having on his son. He admitted it had been a mistake wanting to get him involved in the first place. And I said that the best thing for Helmuth's peace of mind would be to drop the case altogether and never mention it again. Maybe then, with time, Helmuth would calm down. Or maybe not. No, probably not. I told him I was not too sure of myself in these matters.

"Drop the case altogether? You can't be serious. I could take the whole thing somewhere else, of course, do it out of house. But give it up entirely? Just because of the boy and his whims?"

"It's more than just a whim. It's a problem of trust, in you and the entire world. That's his main problem."

"Fine," said Herr Wellner. "I'll talk to my lawyer, and to Helmuth. I'll take the files and have the work done elsewhere. Neither you nor Helmuth will have anything to do with it anymore. Maybe then he'll forget the whole thing."

"It won't be that simple," I said.

I explained to Helmuth that everything was different now, that the two of us would no longer have anything to do with his father's legal case. His father told him it was a misunderstanding. He had no intention of initiating any legal proceedings. The whole thing had been more of a hobby for him. And as far as the family estate was concerned, it had nothing to do with the ferry but originated from completely different sources. All of this was untrue, of course. I knew that Herr Wellner was determined to pursue the case, but I couldn't possibly compromise him in the eyes of his son, who was still suspicious despite all the efforts to persuade him otherwise. He just kept repeating: "How come . . . I become gardener's boy . . . Earn my keep."

His plan to work as a gardener had fully taken possession of him, and it was best for me to play along.

"That gardening thing is actually not a bad idea," I said. "I know a gardener out at the Baumgarten. Herr Wondrak. He was in the army with my father. The Degenfeld regiment in Pilsen. I could have a word with him."

"Baumgarten," cried Helmuth enthusiastically, "go there now . . . right now!"

The vast public park known as the Baumgarten was located on the outskirts of town. In the high, brightly colored treetops, autumn was making its music. The flowerbeds were resplendent with dahlias and asters. A summer palace in Biedermeier Gothic style presided amiably over an English garden. The gardener Wondrak was not in his little green cottage. He was running errands in town, his wife said, and would only be back in the evening. We should come back tomorrow. The delay was fine by me, since I feared I'd been a bit indiscriminate by agreeing so quickly to Helmuth's gardener plan. And so we continued our walk in the park. Carriages and horsemen wound their way through the alleys, recalling the Parisian watercolors of Guys. I had seen these in the art magazine *Kunst und Künstler*. In the beer garden a military band was playing their last piece, no. 12, "The Gladiator March." Helmuth wanted to know every tree, bush and flower.

"Be patient," I told him. "Your father and your mother love you very much. And you and I are friends, aren't we?"

"How come," was all he said, and since I knew that, coming from Helmuth, this wasn't always a question, I didn't bother to answer.

That evening I explained to Frau Carola that Helmuth

wished to work as a gardener and that I knew a certain Herr Wondrak who might be able to help, and as usual she was very understanding. "It's probably the best you could do. It will take his mind off things, and might even be the answer we've been looking for. We should have thought of something like this sooner. Of course we'd pay the gardener on a regular basis for letting Helmuth work. And part of that money he could give to Helmuth as wages."

Admittedly, this well-meaning scheme made me profoundly nervous. On the other hand, there was no reason to expect Herr Wondrak to take on an apprentice right now, in the fall, when he presumably didn't need one and when Helmuth, despite his best intentions, would most likely end up causing more harm than good. We couldn't keep Herr Wondrak in the dark about this. On the other hand, Helmuth would have to be paid for his work. That was what mattered to him. He would then use his earnings, or so he told me, to pay his parents for room and board. After some back and forth and a visit by Frau Carola to Herr Wondrak, the latter showed himself willing to take on a new apprentice. My task was to accompany Helmuth to the Baumgarten each morning, then pick him up in the afternoon and spend another two hours with him until evening.

Helmuth was very hard-working, indeed downright enthusiastic if not a bit overzealous. He cleared away withered flowerbeds and dug them up with a shovel, hauled wheelbarrows of humus, pruned bushes, raked up fallen leaves. He watered plants in the long greenhouse, helped transplant others from small to bigger containers, and endeavored to make himself useful wherever he could. Lacking as he did a delicate touch, he often ended up breaking pots or would shatter a pane of glass with a sudden, unexpected movement. He was deeply distressed whenever this happened, but Herr Wondrak would kindly reassure him; the damages were duly noted and reimbursed. Wondrak was a benevolent older man who oversaw a good number of other garden workers. He was shrewd enough to keep them away from Helmuth whenever possible, and had no doubt hinted at the peculiar nature of the case. Yet the other gardeners, for most of the day, were scattered throughout the spacious park, going about their various tasks, and only encountered Helmuth during their lunch break. And then they treated him with a certain reserve, as I noticed on one occasion, were always good-natured and considerate, teasing him in a friendly way, which he gladly put up with and doled out in kind. They called him "Pozor," a Czech expression meaning "Watch out!" and which Helmuth luckily never held against them but took to be a reference to his being a novice.

His mood quickly and noticeably brightened, and in the hours we spent together in the afternoon he lectured me about the meaning and importance of his work and the characteristics and peculiarities of the plants he worked with. "Protect the plants . . . Look after the plants . . . repot . . . water. Growing . . . How come . . . sun . . . water . . . soil . . . warmth." And he started writing poems again.

Tree above ground
leaf, branch and sun
under the ground

down there there's none.
Up high green leaves
bare brown low down
two different lives
in root and crown.

On his first payday he raced straight home, so fast I could barely keep up with him. He spread the money out on the table so Frau Carola could see it. Two ten-crown notes, eight one-crown pieces and two crowns in nickel and copper coins he'd exchanged on the way home to make it look like as much as possible. He laid it all out, neatly arrayed. Half the table was covered with it.

"Wonderful," said Frau Carola, delighted with her son. "That's much more than your room and board costs. You've still got five whole crowns left over."

Another white lie. But I didn't say a thing, what with the pained expression on Frau Carola's face and an aged look in her eyes that was somehow deeply moving. My lips were sealed. The web of the unspoken, all the things withheld and distorted surrounding Helmuth's life, was too dense and intertwined, and I myself was inescapably woven into it.

Herr Wellner couldn't help giving me the occasional update on the progress he was making with his lawsuit. His lawyer had entrusted two clerks with the task of working out the details. Experienced typists worked tirelessly copying out the trove of documents dating back multiple centuries. Photographic copies were made, trips to various cities undertaken, church records, land registers, inheritance contracts, estate deeds, conveyance documents and other evidence began piling up in a big archive in which three doctors *utriusque juris* — of canon and civil law — were now employed. But the costs of this legal work had soon become so exorbitant that even the resources of Herr Wellner were severely strained. And you could see it in his face. Behind the glimmer of satisfaction over the progress his legal stratagems were making I thought I detected a sense of anxiety, for he could presumably no longer live off the interest of his capital and had to tap into this capital itself — the last thing any propertied individual wants to do. I had an inkling of this state of affairs. Frau Carola once sighed when talking about the high costs of living, something that never would have occurred to her before. But her husband wouldn't let up. To him the case was like a mistress for whom no sacrifice was deemed too great.

Despite the many precautions taken, it was almost inevitable that the public would catch wind of the case Herr Wellner was preparing against City Hall as ever new details were leaked. Too many people were involved in gathering the documents to guarantee complete discretion until the claim was filed. The question was even raised at a City Council meeting if anyone was aware of a lawsuit being prepared that was seeking compensation for damages and that intended to curtail important transportation rights of citizens. Wellner had not yet been mentioned by name, but the well-informed no doubt knew what and who it was all about. Some city councilors viewed the affair as pure querulousness, a ridiculous quibble; others put on a grave face; still others were convinced that in a public affair of such magnitude a private plaintiff could not prevail over the common law of an entire municipality. The man was a legal fanatic, they said, a modern-day Kohlhaas who didn't know the difference between being right and insisting on one's right, and who in any case wasn't quite right in the head. Let him operate his ferry if that's what he wants. But the bridge? Eventually a local paper ran a short notice mentioning Jakob Wellner by name.

Every crisis of human affairs manifests itself simultaneously at multiple points of the organism of being. The day that news appeared in the paper I asked Herr Wondrak about Helmuth, to no avail. He hadn't returned to work after his lunch break. I asked the other gardeners about him, if he'd said anything to them or complained about something. Their answers were evasive at first. Finally it came to light that some of them had been teasing Helmuth at lunchtime, innocently, of course, and without intending any harm. One of them had happened to be reading the paper and said: "Pozor, you're famous. I just read something about your old man." And how did they know his name, I asked, if they only ever called him "Pozor"?

"Precisely because of that," said Herr Wondrak. "He told them himself a few days ago. He didn't want to be called Pozor anymore. I'm not Pozor, he cried, I'm a good worker, I'm Helmuth Wellner. No secret lasts forever."

And that was how he learned his father was still pursuing the case. But that alone was not the reason for his disappearance. Things were in fact much worse. He had gone straight to Wondrak's cottage after being teased about the notice in the paper. Wondrak wasn't home, just his wife, and Helmuth vehemently demanded from her that his wages be paid out immediately. The woman naturally refused, saying she had nothing to do with such things. And before she knew it she let slip that, anyhow, Helmuth's father had not yet sent the money for his wages.

"Women. They can't keep their mouths shut," said Wondrak. "I feel pretty bad about it. The boy ran away and hasn't come back yet. But there's no use getting worked up. He'll turn up before long. A boy like that is like a cat: he'll find his way back when he's hungry."

The Baumgarten, on its northern edge, is bordered by the banks of the Moldau which, after making a wide loop through friendly meadows and gentle slopes, continues on its northward route until, by the little town of Melnik, known for its vineyards, it eventually joins the Elbe.

The Moldau originates in the south from two little rivulets in the depths of the Bohemian Forest, winding its way from there toward the small town of Oberplan, where for a brief stretch it makes a U-turn, forming the shape of a heart, which a great poet and native son fondly and wistfully memorialized in his work.

The silvery cadences, the chords arising out of them, the cheerful, scrappy melodies of this river produce an unforgettable music of symphonic polyphony that is echoed by the river banks, by the entire countryside around it, the solitary farms and hamlets, the villages, the ancient towns, and the castles steeped in lore and legend that play an important, indeed a sacred role in the folklore, the history, the literature of the land and its nations and peoples, from Witiko to the warriors of God, and later on, too.

In the grand coordinate system of watercourses that holds together Bohemia, this continent within a continent, the Moldau is the heroic river of fate given over entirely to its homeland.

At the threshold of the capital it swells to a mighty breadth beneath the Vyšehrad fortress, gathers the hundred spires above its shores, and mirrors the primeval maternal promises of a mythical, stellar glory. The city's bridges firmly hold these shores together, not merely to connect them but as if they wanted to prevent the banks from drifting further apart and to secure the river's depth.

This depth conceals a great deal.

The day Helmuth Wellner disappeared and was nowhere to be found was a turning point in my life for another reason as well. Late at night, returning home from my long and fruitless searches and queries, from my hopeless talks with his grieving parents, from my futile visits to hospitals and police stations, I found my draft notice. The war, which was now in full gear, no longer allowed me to take part directly in the fate of the Wellners. All I learned was that Jakob Wellner never initiated the lawsuit he had built up with so much painstaking effort, and that not long after the events related here he and his wife both died.

In later years, while strolling through the Baumgarten one day, I chanced upon an aging Wondrak. He was busy with some workers removing a rotten maple.

"A pity to see the old tree go," I said.

"You say the tree's a pity? Losing a good person, now that's a pity. The tree might fall on top of someone."

They had slung a rope around the branches of its still leafy crown and sawed a notch into its trunk. Two workers pulled the rope from a distance, and the trunk began to lean. An almost human groaning was audible from its foliage, growing louder and louder. The base of its majestic root system remained silent like gray granite. Then came a last, hefty tug on the rope.

"Pozor!" cried Wondrak.

That means: Watch out! It also means: Be careful. And it also means: Attention. The meaning of a single word can be manifold and momentous, and one would do well to always keep that in mind.

SHRINE

Weissenstein Karl

"I, Weissenstein Karl, proclaim to the Universe, to the edifice of the world . . ."

"*From* the Universe, Weissenstein, from the edifice of the world . . ."

"Don't interrupt me, please. Part of me is up there in celestial spheres, the other part down here on Earth. I, Weissenstein Karl, speaking to and from the Cosmos, would now like to dictate the story of my life to you. You remember that the late Franz Werfel urged you many years ago, from California, to write my story. That was right after he himself had published an essay on me in English. Never would I have thought they'd be talking about me in a foreign language, and overseas at that."

"I told Werfel to talk to Chaplin about you, as a character I mean. But Werfel wrote back: 'Chaplin *is* Weissenstein. So we can't really expect him to play Weissenstein, can we.'"

"But Werfel wasn't satisfied with the sketch he had made of me. He wrote to you that you should erect a better monument to me."

"Those were his words."

"So why not allow me to help you? Especially considering some of the other misconceptions that people in the literary world seem to have about me. For instance, the claim that I was killed in the First World War trying to save a detachment of captured Russians I was supposedly in charge of just behind the front lines. You should know that's nonsense."

"Obviously, since you paid me a visit in 1922, four years after the war."

"You see. It was on your wedding day, I came to congratulate you. In the apartment you were renting in Karolinenthal."

"From Frau Bauer. You even brought us a wedding gift."

"In person. Half a roast goose and a group of porcelain figures, Old Bohemian style."

"Representing the amorous entanglement of a shepherd with a shepherdess. Even back then I said: 'Weissenstein, you shouldn't have.'"

"But now you see it was good that I did, to prove that I was still alive, even if only temporarily, but almost another five years all the same. I even worshipped a girl in those years, who unfortunately came to a tragic end, despite her being from a good family. I'll have more to say about her later on. She had a very common name, which is why I called her Philomena."

"Yes. I recall your writing me a postcard that said: 'Warmest regards from my ever faithful Philomena, although you've never met.' I do remember that."

"Let me start at the beginning, please. But what is the beginning? It doesn't seem right to begin the story of your life with your mother in childbed, which you know about from hearsay at best, but with the moment in which you first fully grasped the necessity and the futility, the finality and the impermanence of life. You're astonished by the way I speak? I always spoke two ways, people just didn't notice.

And over time my manner of expression has only become more refined.

"Anyway, the moment I'm referring to came when I was in my twenties, in a Prague coffeehouse, you remember the Edison. I was hungry and utterly exhausted, having made the last leg of my trek from Tschaslau, the long road from Jirny to Prague, without a bite to eat. I was totally broke. But I entered the coffeehouse anyway, or, rather, I dragged myself up the stairs, because it was on the second floor, to at least sit down for a while then wait for a miracle to happen. Why, in my tiredness, I decided to climb a flight of stairs instead of entering a street-level café, which would have been much more convenient, belongs to the inexplicable realm of providence.

"The waiter asked what I wanted to order and I proudly answered I was waiting for a gentleman, which was obviously a lie but actually turned out to be true. I just didn't know at the time who that gentleman might be. The waiter placed a glass of water in front of me while simultaneously, with an elegant flourish, serving a sandwich to a customer at the neighboring table.

"I call it my sandwich of fate, for the sight of it determined my future and somehow made me a poet. There it sat, enthroned on the plate, salami-red and pale-cheese-yellow, silvery reflections of ocean spray in the upside-down sardines in oil, matted emerald-cucumber green, curly-anchovy brown, above it the added heliotrope of a caper, a wonder of nature, selected by the profoundly experienced chef de cuisine from all around the world, from the sloping, sonorous meadows of Switzerland, from the blueness of the Mediterranean, from the puszta of Hungary, the wheat fields of Bohemia, the olive groves of Provence, ripened and purified in the light of rotating suns, formed from the wisdom and toil of many nations and generations. The world thus lay before me, gloriously aromatic, calmly waiting for eye and hand to seize it, for the voracious appetite of a moneyed customer, prepared for imminent transformations just as it itself had emerged from transformations, waiting for this one great moment, the harmonious triumph of colors, shapes and smells.

"I'd never seen the Alps or the sea, never the heights, expanses or depths. I wasn't worthy. But next to it stood the tiny glass of water-clear slivovitz, and I certainly knew what that was, ever since earliest childhood, slivovitz distilled on a farm in a Montenegrin village, intensely fragrant and almost Homeric, that's how I'd put it nowadays, containing as it did the sound of the guzla and the monotonous epic song of the old blind singer from the village square about the heroes on Kosovo field waging their eternal battle. I say this all from today's perspective. Back then, a quarrel about the pernicious effects of alcohol had been the very reason for my penniless flight to Prague. But more about that later. The slivovitz was mocking me now, the towering sandwich and drink accosted my empty stomach with an air of power and invincibility.

"But not just my stomach. Beyond glass, plate and tabletop I saw dancing women, aroused by exotic strains of music, moving, gyrating, vibrating from some secret source. I felt them deep in my ribs. Woman comes from the rib, and so it's there she gets under our skin.

"In this moment of ravenous hunger and agonies of flesh and heart, I felt how alive I was and how much I needed life. I closed my eyes. Darkness surrounded me. In this blackout my entire previous life flickered before my eyes. My childhood in the village watering hole of my father, where alongside the mingled stench of various kinds of hooch there smoldered in a noxious cloud the belches of the drunkards. There the electorate of Potschaplitz would totter, lay and lean about while my father — always sporting a stiff brown derby hat, which in those days was called a 'jackdaw' — served them his liquor, slivovitz, corn schnapps, kummel, bitters, what he referred to as cognac, which was really just grain spirit colored yellow, acrid brandies with the taste of prussic acid or laced with fennel, rum that was oblivious to the existence of sugarcane but was made from spent grain or pomace, which is why it was called 'Prodigal Son.' It smelled like old boots. My father proffered it all with nauseated naturalness, in thick little shot glasses and on credit rather than cash, debtors being the most steadfast drinkers. He used to say, 'Somebody's got to run the joint,' just like the executioner who says, 'Somebody's gotta hang 'em.'

"An exception to this rule was old Kolator, who claimed he was 114 years old and had helped defeat Napoleon as a drummer boy in the Battle of Aspern. He paid by the drink, which annoyed the ones who drank on credit and therefore responded with the hostile assertion that Kolator was not 114 but a mere 113, or some said even just 90 years old. I was rather fond of him, even though one time, when I was seven, he gave me a numbing slap in the face — deservingly, I might add, for I'd kicked him in the shin, deliberately and no doubt painfully. 'What do you think you're doing!' he roared. 'I just wanted to know which one is the peg leg.' 'The other one, you brute,' and then came the slap.

"Apart from that, though, my childhood was certainly no bed of roses. My mother was no longer among the living. My Father's mother lived with us, but she'd always been at odds with my mother. It was this grandmother who raised me, as they say. Her child-rearing consisted of sitting on a footstool, watching my every move and every once in a while shouting, 'Come here!' Then she'd spit on her dirty hanky and wipe some smudge off my cheek. What would grownups say if children did those kinds of things to them? And yet children's saliva is much less sour and smelly, the cheeks of old people much more repugnant. And while she was wiping my grandmother would say, 'You're no Hugatschek, that's for sure.' This Hugatschek, or little Hugo, was another, fabulous grandchild from another son of hers. I only ever saw him once, later on, but he was always held up as a reproach against me.

"There were slaps in the face at every opportunity, even because the teacher had called me astigmatic. At the age of fourteen I was packed off to the district town where I was given room and board with a tailor so I could attend Gymnasium there. The meals consisted mostly of flour-thickened soup and the lodgings were a bed in a drafty corner of the attic. My father hoped to make a doctor out of me. Whether a doctor of law or medicine made no difference to him, just as long as I was a doctor. But already in the very first year I was expelled from every grammar school in the Kingdoms and Lands Represented in the Imperial Council. I had lifted the skirt of the janitor's wife in the hallway and cried out: 'Where's the S? Where's the consonant?' They summoned me to the teachers' council. 'Why did you do that,' the principal barked at me. 'Nouns ending in *s* preceded by a consonant, these are feminine,' I stuttered. 'When you ask him in class he's clueless,' said my Latin teacher. 'We'll have to make an example of him,' explained the principal. Thus, my thirst for practical knowledge was ultimately my undoing. My father gave me a hiding then sent me to apprentice with a glovemaker.

"There, too, the female sex brought misfortune upon me. I was fifteen now. The master's wife made eyes at me, which flattered me enormously. Because, as you know, I've got a scrawny build and — let's be honest — my head is much too big, I've got what they call 'water on the brain.' Aunt Karla — about whom more later — had used the hackneyed words 'It suits you,' but she just didn't know what to say. The glovemaker's wife found it easy to seduce me. I wasn't the only one she had, but I was within easy reach. And so, while I didn't learn how to make gloves, I did get a good lesson in life. It was odd enough. The glovemaker knew exactly what was going on but didn't say a thing for the longest time. Then one day after dinner he up and stabbed his wife with an awl without so much as a quarrel — we'd had tripe soup that was much too spicy. Maybe that's what riled him up. He didn't have a single harsh word for me, but simply sent me to the police to report what had happened. The police sergeant said, 'That's impossible.' The news made him uneasy, since he too had counted among the friends of the glovemaker's wife. Now, whether he liked it or not, he had to go and arrest her husband. It ended with a huge trial, where I testified as a witness.

"'Did you have relations with the murdered woman?' asked the judge.

"'No. But I did when she was alive.'

"Everyone laughed. 'Don't ridicule the court,' the judge snapped at me.

"'I'm telling the truth, like I swore I would,' I said. And believe me, I wasn't being cheeky. All the same, that was the first time my father swore he was going to cut me out of his will.

"After the trial, I spent a while accompanying a trader to fairs, helping him sell his novelties. One was a threading machine. I learned the sales pitch by heart, and could rattle it off like a phonograph record. 'Mother comes home from the fields. Her eyes are weak and wearied from work. She wants to thread a needle but, try as she might, the poor woman misses every time, she can't get the thread through the eye of the needle. But those who have my threading machine simply take the needle and thread, and voilà, it's threaded just like that. This threading machine cost one crown and fifty hellers at the exhibition in New York. Today it's affordable to everyone for the low price of just twenty hellers. Lucky buyers receive fifty meters of white and fifty meters of black thread, altogether one hundred meters of thread, free and postage-paid, along with twenty-five sewing needles, a bobbin and a thimble.' Using this prepared speech, which I could deliver in Czech or German at will, I wound up being hugely successful at every fair between Königgrätz and Trautenau.

"The job had something of the circus life, that is to say of real life, makeshift in every detail, and I probably would have kept at it if the fair-trader himself hadn't driven me away. Every four weeks he'd have a religious fit and claim he was one of the Silesian Brethren, which was pretty bad for business, and then he would start fasting and forced me to fast along with him, saying, 'Young man, many things happen to you but you yourself make nothing happen. Go! Don't let me see you here again.'

"And so I left him and went to Pardubitz, where I took up at first with a typewriter salesman, who threw me out just two days later when, regrettably, I'd taken his typewriters apart and no one could put them back together again, since I'd hopelessly mixed up the parts of different models. It was a stretch, though, to claim that my next boss, the jeweler Patsch, dismissed me for crushing one of his diamonds. I left on my own accord, mainly because I found his customers depressing. Because it was right about then that I began to devour the Church Fathers and all kinds of socialist tracts. I had an acquaintance in Pardubitz, a law clerk named Adamek, who lent or procured me hundreds of books. It was he who laid the foundation of my education.

"But fate caught up with me in Pardubitz in the form of a horseless, driverless cart that began rolling down a steep street and ran me down, because God so willed it. They knew who the cart belonged to, but the man was far too powerful a figure in Pardubitz for anyone to dare approach him about the matter.

I'd broken a number of bones, so they put me in the hospital and, since I was still a minor, shunted me off when I was three-quarters healed to my father's drinking hole in Potschaplitz. So there I was again, asking myself, 'What's the point of it all, how often does one have to fail?' 'Help out in the back with the bottling and labeling,' my father ordered. He was the type who liked to give orders. The back room was one big racket, where he fiddled of course with the quality but also with the quantity and price. Now, you might say that cheating on a thing so contemptible somehow balances out in the end. But a jumble of lies like this was nothing for a young man like me. My father's whole business, with all the drunkards, and indeed my very parentage sickened me more than ever. And so one Sunday evening, when the taproom was full of half or fully intoxicated customers, I leapt up onto the table and began to hold forth on the evils of alcohol and alcoholism. I let each and every drunkard have it, one after the other, accused the one of letting his wife and children starve at home, the other of boozing away half his potato harvest, a third for giving himself a dilated heart which would lead to convulsions and a horrible death, and announced that all of them together were godforsaken slaves of a perfidious tavern-owner who cheated them left and right and happened, on top of it all, to be my very own father. Only after this tirade did my father yank me down from the table and give me two tremendous blows making it clear to me once and for all that I was banished from hearth and home, and that my inheritance, if there ever was one, would be going to the much-lauded Hugatschek for sure, whose shining example had been held up to me ever since my diaper days. This is how I came to Prague — on foot and without a heller to my name.

"Prague had always been the city of my dreams. 'You have to go to Prague,' Adamek had always advised me, 'you can go a long way there. The Czechs and Germans, Christians and Jews are always at each other's throats. The coffeehouses have newspapers from all around the world. And there's a butcher's shop next to every coffeehouse. There's always a butcher next-door in Prague. And everyone is gorging themselves as if it were doomsday. Everything's on display in Prague. At the Pištěk Theater you can see what things were like in the court of Louis XIV, with all the whores and everything. And up on Hradschin, when you're down in the dumps, you can view the intact body of Blessed Sister Electa or bearded Saint Starosta. Then when you're in Lesser Town, go to Café Radetzky. It's cozy. The coffee might be made of *lógr*, as the Czechs call the dregs of boiled chicory, but if it's kind of true of Café Radetzky what the Viennese poet said of the field marshal of the same name, "In your camp (*Lager*) is Austria," then in your *lógr* is Austria, too.'

"And so I went to Prague and was sitting, faint with hunger, not in Café Radetzky but at least in Café Edison. I can't say how long the swoon I was in lasted, but I know my entire previous life passed before my inner eye. It probably lasted just a few minutes, or maybe even less. Because when I came to, the gentleman next to me had not even started eating his sandwich. Through the crystal-clear lenses magnifying his eyes he observed me with a bluish-cool gaze, behind whose ironic luster lay just a hint of smugness, still like standing water. Again, don't be surprised by my choice of words, I've been carefully polishing this sentence during all the long years I've contemplated this gaze over and over again. You'd be mistaken to think that a person with such a look in his eyes, and about to devour a lavish sandwich, would be incapable of doing a good deed. Because without my uttering a single word he said, 'I understand your predicament,' and handed me a florin. 'My future and the emancipated slaves will thank him,' I thought when he said it, and immediately ordered an appetizer sandwich just as fancy as his. It was in this manner — and not as a result of the anarchist Vohryzek, who appeared on the scene much later, and whom Herr Werfel gave an account of in his essay — that I became enthralled to literature. The giver of the florin was none other than engineer and architect Herr Feldscharek in person, a close acquaintance of the famed 'friend of the world,' of the cosmic poet Fuchs, of the doctor of exalted emotions Brod, and then some, including you yourself. But in the case of poets, the factual is always a function of the categorical. For every fact, every thought they write or utter there are always two or three they keep to themselves or allow to perish inside them. In short, their invisible kingdom is always greater than the visible one.

"A florin or two crowns used to go a long way back in Old Austria. I not only paid my bill but had my hair cut by Rýchlik, the barber on Hibernergasse, I saw the matinée show — it was Saturday — on a standing-room ticket at the variety theater, where Sylvester Schäffer cut in half a woman suspended in midair, I watched Sacco the hunger artist in his glass case on the twelfth day of his fast, I ate three Italian sausages afterward, with horseradish, at Ugge's butcher shop, then, in the evening, I showed up at Café Arco, Herr Feldscharek having asked me to come and where he introduced me to the caryatids of Prague literature. They gave me ties, stand-up collars and vests as presents, found me odd jobs, paid for my coffees and pastries, and also expanded my knowledge. And you know already (it's been in print) how I rose to become a secret editor of the great Expressionist publisher, an *éminence grise* so to speak, who relieved these gentlemen of letters of their reading load and frequently offered my appraisal too, trusting as they did my unbroken instincts. Soon I began to write my own poetry.

"Being an Expressionist was a lot of fun. I wrote under a pseudonym for publications called *Action* and *Storm*, *Saturn* and *Revival*, *Sickle* and *Flute*, *Red Earth* and *New Pathos*. I was many poets at once. Half of Expressionism was actually my doing, people just don't know it, and it'll never be possible to prove it for certain, because I myself don't recall anymore to what extent, from time to time, I was Sternheim or Ehrenstein or Paul Adler. I shared the editor's life in Leipzig and Hellerau with the gentlemen from the publishing house. It's a slice of literary history, you have to admit. But it did have its drawbacks. How often did Paul Adler wake me in the Hellerau night at three or four in the morning. 'Get up, Weissenstein. I need inspiration. We have to take a walk.' I got up and slipped on three sweaters — poor bastards like me have to wear their clothing in layers — and we stumbled through the night, over hill and over dale, over ditch and over hedge and into the morning light, and when I was on the verge of collapsing Adler exclaimed: 'Never mind, Weissenstein, that's life. One seeks eternity, but the search is always provisional.' So on we went, and each time I stumbled he cried: 'Enjoy the fresh air, Weissenstein! God created fresh air and pure water, but man produced foul smells and well poisoning.' Or he said: 'That's the whole point. You have to feel that you're alive. Life consists mainly of being alive.' These nightly heats gave rise to many beautiful books. But let's return to Prague.

"They say I envied the penmen their girlfriends. They portray me as some kind of moocher who let them support him, a clown they kept to make fun of. Outwardly it may have seemed that way, and it may have been true to a certain extent. But why should I have envied the writers their girlfriends? After all, I went almost daily to Vlasta, who was strong as a Bohemian Amazon of yore, with her innocent gaze and her wealth of life experience. And, like the poets, I took what came to me of its own accord. I'll have more to say about Vlasta later. But first a few words about the war. The war and literature — those were the two big universal things I took part in. They drafted me into the Austrian army and the literary men had to laugh, and you too laughed, and I did too, since it didn't bode well for an empire that relied on a person like me to defend it, what with my pitiful constitution and my unmistakable hydrocephalus. At the same time I was scared. Not fearful for my own life or well-being, but scared by the possibility of being forced to annihilate or even just endanger another life. I did everything not to be sent to the front. And when they made me a titular corporal anyway and I reported to receive my commission, I tossed — out of despair more than courage — a handful of stars at the commanding officer, stars like the kind they used as insignia, one for a private, two for a corporal, and so on. I wanted to show my contempt for everything related to the military. The consequences of my protest were bad and good at the same time. I was naturally placed under strict arrest, but could basically consider myself lucky, since they took me more for a fool than a rebel. A fool for not wanting to become a titular corporal! One day in lock-up, I asked to speak to the Catholic chaplain. He actually came, and sat down on my plank bed next to me. 'What is it you want?' he asked. 'You don't look very Catholic to me.'

"'Father, I think I'm a Christian.'

"'It's easy to think so, but harder to be one.'

"'I'm not even lying,' I said, 'or only a little.'

"'That's a good start,' remarked the chaplain, 'but wait till the lie is gone completely, then you can call on me again.'

"I never got that far, but it was surely the chaplain who effected my early release and had me transferred to Prague's commissariat office — 'garrison rations' in army-speak.

"There I was assigned to the victuals department, and in no time at all — even though I was still a titular corporal — I occupied a position of power about which Herr Pollak, the bank clerk, once remarked that it would have been the ideal subject for the Spanish painter Goya, who should have depicted me in his *Desastres de la Guerra*. For amidst a general scarcity of basic foodstuffs I was in a position to procure for gluttonous officers and their families such things as rice, lentils, coffee or — by virtue of my influence with the meat department — bacon, smoked meats, sausages, in short almost everything that was otherwise impossible to obtain in the latter phases of the war. I was proof that man is much more compellingly at the mercy of the little potentates than of the great powers. I imagined how villainously I could have abused my powers. But the mere thought of it frightened me, and in retrospect I can truly say: this was my most virtuous hour. I didn't let anyone grease my palm. I simply had the good fortune to be able to dole out privileges, and this to individuals who were much higher up than me and had money at their disposal.

"I knew exactly where in the warren of giant warehouses lay a hidden sack of coarsely ground wheat flour, a tub of marinated eel, or a crate of Dutch cocoa. Staff officers, even a major general, acted extremely friendly toward me, because I'd found a way for their families to occasionally get their hands on a forbidden liter of milk. There was milk whose existence was known to only a few insiders. Each day requisitioned cows were driven to slaughter. You could hear from afar their frantic bellowing when the smell of the slaughterhouse reached their nostrils. They bellowed a requiem for themselves and for Austria. Before being slaughtered they were hastily milked one last time. Too little milk to distribute equitably, but enough to be corrupt. I received my cut of the milk because I knew how the sergeants at the weighing station cheated, doctoring the live weight of the animals and going halves with the cattle dealers who drove them in. Whenever the cow was on the scale, the cattle driver standing next to it would put one foot on the scale too and, just at the moment of weighing, unnoticeably lift his other foot, thus adding his own weight to that of the cow. I'd been observing this for a while from my cashier's office. So I said to the weighmaster, 'I've got a perfect view from my window.' — 'You want milk?' he answered.

"I soon learned that the meat in the storerooms got lighter from drying out and that dozens of kilos were being siphoned off when doing the daily accounts. The loss figures were totally arbitrary, for who could or would even want to reweigh all those mounds of meat every day? 'You want meat?' asked the man from the meat warehouse. And so I had milk and meat. Knowledge is power. I could allocate benefits on the quiet, not only to officers' wives but also to the needy, whom I knew more about than other people did, and also to the poets and artists at Café Arco. For I also had something to offer the artists, something more important than meat or victuals. At a time when painter's canvas was in short supply I discovered in the corner of a remote warehouse a few dozen empty tea crates, each one made of six immaculate, smooth plywood panels of one square meter a piece. No one seemed to care about them. I spent whole nights carefully prying them apart and gave the panels away to the painters. Many a Czech cubist painting was done on those plywood panels. It was my proudest moment. But this, too, was only temporary. I had to reckon with getting hanged before long, because some ridiculous fanatic had taken to exposing our outfit's benevolent double dealing. It was then that world history along with the attendant collapse of the monarchy ultimately came to my aid. An entire empire had to go under just so the weighmaster, the man from the meat warehouse, myself, and a handful of other companions could get off scot-free.

"By that time I'd been going to Vlasta for quite a while already. I had seen her in one of Prague's many murky houses with interior passageways, where she lived together with a girlfriend in a ground-floor room accessible from the street. In passing I'd peeped through the window, and there she stood in front of a mirror wearing only her undies, looking heavenly and earthly at once. In the mirror she saw me peeping, and without even turning around she beckoned and drew me into her room, magnetically as it were, with the movement of her index finger. She eyed me from top to toe. 'Well, I never,' she said, laughing, 'and in a uniform, at that! I'd do it with you for a knockwurst, and would even give you a bite of it.' My hydrocephalus didn't bother her. Later I procured a steady supply of Imperial and Royal knockwurst for her. She was cheerful and rather candid when talking about her line of business. 'Some intellectual type was here with pince-nez and briefcase . . .' . . . 'a cabinet official with cotton in his ears. And I say to him: Come on, first take off your glasses. And he says: But then I won't see a thing. Left me a copy of *Piquant World*. I had no idea such garbage even existed.' She had no eduction but was very particular about cleanliness. She hated ambiguity. Each week she went to Dr. Koňas and would talk about the marvels and the glories of his office, with its giant set of antlers on the wall and an oleograph depicting Hus before the Council of Constance. Her girlfriend,

Fanynka, who withdrew discreetly whenever I was there, came from the suburb of Karolinenthal and Vlasta claimed to have straightened her out, since 'those Karlín girls like to drop their stockings,' as she put it.

"Vlasta had a strong sense of social awareness. In the struggle of nations she took no sides. She had a certain regional patriotism, the kind I've heard existed in Bohemia before the year 1848. Often enough during the war, when one of the many victories of Imperial and Royal troops was reported, she would say by way of suggestion: 'Come up to the Castle with me, to celebrate the brotherhood of nations!' I had the vague suspicion, however, that these displays of brotherhood attracted her mainly because they often ended in free-for-alls. With the proclamation of the Republic, Vlasta became a zealous Czech, albeit a very liberal one. 'Germans are people too, and I should know,' she said. That was Vlasta, and I still have plenty to say about her. But I can't do that until after I've talked about Aunt Karla, for fates and events are intertwined. From Aunt Karla the threads lead to another soul, and from there right back to Vlasta.

"Even my grandmother in Potschaplitz used to drop vague hints about Aunt Karla. She was an 'aunt' who was somehow related by marriage. Her husband was a professional pool shark and, being a pioneer of the art, had gone overseas to make his fortune. Karla, for her part, ran a shop in Prague for lady's hats on Eisengasse. I'd forgotten all that long ago. It all came back to me, though, indeed it came to my rescue, the day they marked the victorious revolution by toppling the Marian column on Old Town Square. I was grumbling in the middle of a crowd that knocking down the Virgin Mary doesn't prove a thing when a group of raving patriots began to chase me. I fled through nearby Eisengasse, into the passageways through its buildings, escaping from my pursuers in zigzag fashion, before ending up right back on Eisengasse and running headlong through a shop door just as its iron shutters came clattering down behind me. The woman running the shop was just about to close for the day when I came hurtling through her door. In the room behind the shop, a spirit burner was at work frying up something oniony. The startled woman regarded me and then said, 'May God punish me if that isn't the spitting image of a Potschaplitzer standing before me!' I heard the word Potschaplitz and was suddenly transformed. This corpulent, aunt-like woman, ladies' hats in a glass display case, the name Potschaplitz — in a flash I knew where I was and so I revealed my identity. 'Resembles his father to a T,' she cried, 'come here and let me look at you, what do you do, what's your business?' When in doubt, it's always best to call yourself a writer. 'You don't say! So you're a poet, a musician, an actor,' and so on, whatever rolled off her tongue. 'An artist, it doesn't matter.'

"Meanwhile someone knocked at the rear exit. 'Don't worry,' my aunt reassured me, 'it's just an old customer of mine, Frau Saftová. She always uses the back door. I was beginning to wonder why she hadn't come yet for this year's hat.' She turned off the flame under her spleen roast and introduced me to the lady, who ran the biggest stall on Obstmarkt. 'Here are the latest models. The one with the water lily I wouldn't recommend. Try this one here with black heron feathers made of genuine cellulose. How youthful you look in it!' Another half a dozen hats were tried on, but in the end she took the one with the tuft of heron feathers. After Frau Saftová had paid, without haggling over the price by the way, my aunt turned the spirit burner on again and invited me to supper. 'I always eat here before going home. It's too much of a hassle at home.' She served and sang:

Only
for nature had she
sympathy,
under trees
sweetly dreaming,
loved Countess
Melanie.

"'Melanie' came as a kind of surprise ending, and my aunt accompanied the unusual name with a sweeping flourish of the hand, in which she brandished a fork with skewered spleen roast. 'I'll eat standing up today,' she sighed, 'Sometimes I have a hard time settling my backside into a chair. So that was the Saftová woman. The women all come to me for their Sunday hats, even the pot-and-pan vendors and the slipper sellers from Kohlmarkt. Reliable clientele, I tell you, conservative too. Come back next Saturday at the same time. We'll go up to my place. When I say "next Saturday" I mean this Saturday. What you call "next Saturday" I call the Saturday after next. And be careful in the meantime. Young Hammerschlag got mixed up with a girl from the street and the next day he was dead. Be patient and I'll fix you up with a nice girl from a good family.'

"But back then when Vlasta and Aunt Karla entered my life, and thanks to them Irma too, whom I called Philomena, I was already suffering from the pangs of my multiple existence, which had actually begun in the realm of the Expressionists. I was a Jew and a Christian, a Czech and a German, I was Anton Kuh and Egon Erwin Kisch, Werfel and Rilke, I was you, too, whether you believe it or not. There were times when I suddenly escaped from myself and delivered a speech to an assembly of workers from a platform in a beer garden: 'The organized masses will rise up and destroy their enemy. No more kings, or emperors, or popes!' But while I was speaking I slipped out of my skin again and was suddenly Rabbi Reach, debating at a table in Café Arco with Rabbi Knöpfelmacher about whether or not God was so almighty that He could cancel out His own almightiness. In states like that I had a tremendous knowledge and no inkling of where it came from. I had Kuh's quirks, wore a monocle and shrieked in his squeaky falsetto: 'The downfall of the West is reflected in the fact that bad plays are being performed too well and bad music is being played too well.' As Kisch I commanded Red Guards, cigarette in mouth, and called for the storming of the Vienna Banking Association. And as Urzidil, pardon my saying so, I plunged with all the damned into the depths of the Last Judgment, and had the feeling that you yourself, or Ernst Weiss, the doctor, or Ludwig Winder, the editor, or whomever I felt I was at the moment, in reality didn't exist at all and were only there through me, in me. A monster symphony of the provisional. Every nation, every religion, every party was proven right or wrong in me at some point or another. You'll ask me whether behind it all I was present somehow as Weissenstein Karl, if I ever had a view of myself in all these escapades. No, I tell you. I became the other person entirely. And the fact that they basically often addressed me by the names of the others proves it. 'My respects, Herr Editor-in-Chief,' the headwaiter Poschta greeted me, or 'My respects, Herr Professor!' I see myself being taken for Werfel when I launched into a recitation at the café:

You youthful ones, evenings encircled,
banished into my space, all-orphaned,
how I am your kin!

"Yes, I was Werfel!

"Just don't think that all of that was the bloated consequence of wishful dreaming, because everyone probably has the hidden desire to see himself basking in fame and glory in front of those who look down on him. It wasn't from my sense of nothingness that I tried to be someone. The others were exalted through me, it was me who gave them their full reality, I was Karl Brand, or Hans Gerke, or even you. Indeed, were you always so sure you were Urzidil? Haven't you sometimes felt a little uncanny when someone asks you, 'To whom have I the honor of speaking?' No? How I envy you your security and simplicity!

"'It's old fashioned,' Herr Feldscharek gave me to understand one day when I ran into him on Rittergasse — he avoided acknowledging me on the Graben, since he graded his acquaintances by zones and there were some he talked to on the Graben, others on Bergmannsgasse; I had evidently never made it farther than Rittergasse — 'it's old fashioned,' he said to me, 'to really love a girl like Vlasta. That Wedekind nonsense is so passé.' I received similar warnings from Herr Stein, the lawyer — you know, the Stein who writes those *drames à clef.* You do remember his dramalogues, don't you? 'The cream of society. Tragedy. Dramatis personae: Dr. Paul Fels, a lawyer. Alice Sokaj, a fair lady. Egon Erwin Schick, a reporter. Franz Würfel, a lyric poet. Wanda, an anarchist.' I still remember exactly how you said, 'Stein, if you don't have any ideas, you shouldn't *want* to have any.' So Stein warned me too, and he wasn't alone. Someone who offered me encouragement, on the other hand, was Professor Bachrach. He encouraged everyone in everything. 'Right you are,' he said to me, 'one must take chances in life. You can't hurl bold truths at a world gone rotten then behave like a petty clerk yourself, fearful of losing your pitiful post. Weissenstein, don't worry at all about what others say, abandon any pretense to fame, pay no heed to your enemies, and always remember that three-quarters of everything people say about you are intentional or unintentional lies. Lies, Weissenstein, are endemic to most people. They don't even lie to inflict damage in most cases. They lie for the sake of lying. Or they don't even lie for that. They just lie, period. So if you love this Vlasta, do me a favor and love Vlasta. And, anyway, why am I even saying this? A person is as good as his convictions, not his deeds. Deeds, my dear fellow, are always done under duress. Only convictions are free.' That was Professor Bachrach, who — as you know — was a mathematician and, unfortunately, died far too young.

"So the literary set knew I was going to Vlasta, that I just can't help myself and always have to divulge my innermost feelings, that's the difficult thing about me. Still, I never confessed entirely. Only today, to you, am I doing it. I've told you about my double and multiple lives. I hinted at it once to Aunt Karla in my desperation, but she didn't know what to make of it. It was in the backroom of her shop. She was making fritters from the clusters of elder flowers she'd gathered from the Old Jewish Cemetery, all the while crooning 'A-okay, dining in a chambre séparée.' 'That song will be around for ages,' she said. 'Whad'ya say? Two of you? That's nothing special. Get control of yourself! Everyone has their moments. So there are two of you? Same thing happens in business.' — 'But, Auntie, you can't compare me with Wolf & Schleim or Federer & Piesen. I transform. I stop being Weissenstein Karl, so that often I really don't know anymore if it's me who's transformed into the other or the other who's transformed into me.' And I told her the story of Chuang Tzu's butterfly dream. — 'Yeah, yeah, the ancient Japanese,' said my aunt. 'But it's not as tragic as you think. Every actor goes through that. First he plays Wallenstein, next thing he's Eisenstein. And boys play cops and robbers, first the one then the another, and they do it their whole life long, no matter if they're merchants or ministers. The best thing would be for you to get married. But how are you going to support a wife? Maybe if you had a respectable lady friend you'd finally look for a permanent position. A permanent position, that's the only way. None of this temporary stuff. If you only wanted it, I'd have one for you in a jiffy. Her mother's a widow, *modes robes*, fixed prices.'

"I had never, of course, told Aunt Karla about Vlasta, so one week after her speech she introduced me to a girl whom I henceforth called Philomena. I admit it's a name I partly picked up from reading and partly invented myself. I didn't know what it means, but later someone told me it sounded like nightingales. Anyway, she was delicate and anemic, and evidently subsisted on a diet of Somatose and other iron preparations. It seemed to me that I loved her immediately. I concluded this from the endless stream of nonsense I spluttered and from my shameless boasting, about which I later noted with dismay: 'How, when things get serious, will you ever return to the truth?' But Philomena smiled in such a way that I soon realized she knew exactly what was truth and what was fiction, and that she didn't mind one bit.

"But the fact that I started going with Philomena did not mean I stopped going to Vlasta. I was careful not to touch Philomena, as if it might cause an electric short circuit. I had no built-in fuses at first. Talking, I'd be fine with that, but I had this mammoth skull, my nose was off-center, my ears were as big as my hands, and my eyes were different colors. None of that could be overlooked. We took walks together through the parks of Prague and along the banks of the Moldau, and when I had a little money from running errands or part-timing at Fuchs Funeral Home (*pompes funèbres*), or sometimes just by pumping Aunt Karla, I took a paddle steamer with her out to Kuchelbad or we hiked to the palace-restaurant of Troja. I never subjected Philomena to the critical eyes of the literary men, for nothing seems more ridiculous than a couple unmistakably in love. All the same, I went to Vlasta almost every day and only once a week to Philomena. Neither one knew about the other. But Vlasta had instincts. One time, holding me between her knees like Delilah did with Samson, I grew weak and began to make insinuations. I don't know what made me do it, but it was probably the demon of vanity. Vlasta laughed at first, but then got angry. And she had good reason to do so, she who had been so generous and sincere with me, the hydrocephalic with the elephant ears and crooked nose and with whom she wasn't afraid that he'd have another woman who offered him something more 'refined,' like all the other men who went to her. 'So you're no different than them, the kind who wants to go easy on the other one. The real you, she's too good for that. For Pete's sake, what a brute I've gotten involved with!' She was right. She should have thrown me out then and there. But strangely enough she didn't. She wailed and beat her breast, like in a Greek tragedy. She bawled 'I want to love!' — screamed and howled it in Czech in every possible tone of voice, and, mind you, in Czech it's much more moving than it is in German, it sounds like some kind of folk song. 'How can you love my hydrocephalus?' I asked, and added, 'I'm not worthy of you,' which, true as it was, still sounded like I'd lifted it straight from an opera. We made a huge scene complete with yelling, crying, lamenting and self-incriminations, well into the bed, so that in the end even Fanynka, who was busy in the room next door, was crying and wailing along with us.

"Maybe life and my reading the poets had made such a mess of me that I no longer knew how to act naturally, so that I asked myself with everything and everyone: Is this world real and true, myself included, or is it but a stage? Does it not consist of a million makeshift arrangements running parallel and counter to each other and putting on a grand theater of illusion? Today I'm well aware that this is an ancient philosophical conundrum. But if — as in my case back then — the question isn't posed by a calculating mind but from the pain in all the fibers of existence, then it's no longer simply a question but becomes a source of panic. Only death seems the surest guarantee of life, only dying would make us sure of ourselves. Philomena, who for a while had attended the Wertheimer School of Business, once lectured me on what a check was. I've never actually seen one, but it seems to me that death is akin to endorsing a check; without its endorsement it can't be cashed and hence has no real value.

"You might say my relations with Vlasta should have allowed me to sense now and then, indeed be fully cognizant of the certainty of my life. We think that in moments like these we've seized this eternally fleeting life by the scruff of its neck, if only for an instant. And at first I thought so too. But once she found out about Philomena, the substance of her embraces changed. It was understandable that I couldn't stay away from her. But the fact that she held on to me, there was something mysterious, something sordid and vicious about that. In her overpowering lust lay the will to murder, directed not at me but at the other woman. Smells, body heat, pulse — all of that was just a vicious wish and corrosive venom that entered me only to act upon the unsuspecting, defenseless and gentle Philomena, to gradually and systematically murder her. In this way I became an accomplice of Vlasta, whom each day I felt more compelled to see the more clearly and dreadfully I sensed what was happening. Vlasta's aim — and perhaps she herself didn't know it — was to make me more and more unworthy of Philomena, and thus degrade Philomena in turn, to such an extent that in the end Philomena would not even feel worthy of *me*, and someone who is degraded by me, the most inferior of all living creatures, can only feel the deepest degree of ignominy and by her own lights no longer go on living.

"Now, you might say: 'Weissenstein Karl, you're exaggerating, you're wrestling with phantoms, things are never that complex between two people.' But when little Fritz, in response to the question 'Where's your left ear?' does not simply place his left hand on his left ear but reaches around his head with his right in an utterly impractical way, he only wants to express, quite correctly, that in reality a simple question has no simple answer at all. Because, first of all, the question isn't that simple. And, second, you can't go left except in a roundabout way to the right — and you can't go right except by going left. That's the way of the world, period, and the ways of the Lord aren't wondrous, as they say, but are roundabout and usually unexpected.

"'What? Anything goes with me,' screamed Vlasta, 'but with her you act like Cardinal Skrbenský performing the washing of feet? I'll tell you one thing: You'll ask of her what you ask of me and do with her what you do with me and she'll sweat till she's blue in the face from exertion and act like she's laughing but in the end it'll be like when they weep in Napajedla.' Vlasta took pleasure imagining these things, but each time she lashed out at Philomena she was actually whipping herself, each of her barbs merely dug into her own flesh. 'Is it me you feel or her?' she would whisper. 'Feel her with me and me with her. I can take it. I'm used to it. But she's not.' Some things in this world are so monstrously true that it should be forbidden to utter them. Those who don't want to sabotage life should not seek words for these radical truths. I've been told this is the reason why certain regimes are suspicious of poets. I felt hatred for Vlasta, but in my fits of hatred I grew so close to her that from one encounter to the next I gradually began to transform into her. What I used to experience only with males, the sudden leap into their identity, was happening now to me with Vlasta. So much so, in fact, that only now — as if through her own sensory organs — did I really perceive my dreadfulness and physical repulsiveness, along with the uncanny horror that goes with the female appetite for the lustful devouring and destruction of others.

"By the time this happened, most of the poets I knew had long since scattered and were no longer even in Prague. One, so I heard, was being held under the lead roofs of Venice. Now and then he still sang with great power and splendor. But fame took a toll on him little by little. Another died quietly from afar. I only ever knew him as dying surreptitiously. They transferred his remains and I was there when they buried him. I know that you were there too, but you didn't notice me. No one noticed me, for I hid behind an acacia tree. But at the funeral parlor I work at I was able for one brief second to look the dead man in the face. I felt guilty for being alive. You too? In any event, I didn't want my unworthy person to put in an appearance at his funeral. Someone might have said, 'Are you crazy? In a suit like that?' I always wore a suit 'like that.' I couldn't afford to have my suits made at Metzeles's. My britches were too long and the coat too short, or the britches too short and my coat too long. Nothing ever fit me. Even a made-to-measure suit bought from the finest tailor would have looked ridiculous on me. Even more ridiculous probably. The only one not to criticize or laugh at me would have been the deceased. So I didn't make myself conspicuous, and only approached the grave after everyone else had gone. The only ones left were the burial crew. One of them said, 'They say he was a writer.' — 'He is one,' I answered, 'and will stay one too.' Then I left, and heard one gravedigger say to the other: 'What's it to him?' So the men of letters, as I said, had scattered. Herr Kisch in Berlin was still preparing the world revolution, and had been ever since he was born. In the Bengal lights of inflation, others cast suspiciously large and distorted shadows on the empty projection screen of literature. The light was already pretty skewed. Sometimes it seemed I should leave all my Prague entanglements behind and march off to Berlin as well. But how was I supposed to get there? The Expressionists had brought me to Leipzig once. Now they no longer bothered. They simply said I'd passed away, went missing somewhere in the war, was erased from the book of the living. They didn't even take the trouble to find out if I still existed. I was too unworthy.

"I knew the poets well enough, having transformed into them time and again. Back then the sound of my beating heart was louder than the voices in their heads. Even those who just sat around and had never written a line themselves still carried something heart-like within them, behind their glasses, like Herr Feldscharek, or Herr Fanta, who on the way to the Jewish Burial Society confided to me in a halting voice: 'Sadly, my beloved mother unexpectedly succumbed to a stroke this morning while kneading pastry dough,' and he burst into tears when he added: 'The maid finished making the strudel.' His heart was in what he said, for it was spoken with the dearly departed in mind and directed to the other world. The fellowship of poets was over as far as I was concerned. The war was over too, and new states had emerged. Everyone could now throw his weight around after his own fashion. As the Czechs say: 'The band plays everyone's tune for a while.' Now it was their turn, and so they reclaimed the dance. As Herr Kafka once put it, the commissariat had been my shield that I used to keep the war at bay. From now on I was Weissenstein Karl, it was no mere pseudonym anymore. I was literally a symbol of the world turned topsy-turvy."

"Isn't your name Weissenstein, Weissenstein?"

"The awful thing is: my name is not just Weissenstein. I *am* Weissenstein. Or let's say: I was. And I'm not dictating all of this to you for my own sake, but for the sake of others. Because Aunt Karla always warned me: 'You're a poet. Something of you might remain for posterity. And that's why you should make sure that from everyone you rub shoulders with, the poor devils more than anyone, something of them remains when they're gone. The rich leave their money. It's up to the poets to care for the poor.'

"Neither Aunt Karla nor Vlasta nor Philomena ever knew exactly where I lived back then, and I often didn't know it myself, for I lived in different places, and in fact it was not what they usually call 'living.' Sometimes I'd spend the night at Walter Fürth's, but I couldn't actually sleep there, because he always went on and on the whole night about how much he suffered and was always searching his conscience. 'Woe is me, where did I go wrong? What should I have avoided? Where did I go too far? Who did I offend? In what did I lack humility?' The whole rigmarole of contrition came straight from Dostoevsky, for in reality he did neither too little nor too much but, rather, did nothing at all, and only felt unfortunate because he was so indescribably bored. Sometimes Karl Brand would put me up in his room in Lesser Town. But soon I stopped accompanying him, since I felt I was just interfering with his dying. For a while Herr Doctor Fanta let me sleep in his father's warehouse. It was the chemical storage room of the Unicorn Pharmacy on Old Town Square, filled with the smell of chloroform and the scent of ammonium chloride, its shelves lined with bottles and containers whose labels had skulls and crossbones. Below them loitered rats and mice. There was a sofa, and Fanta appointed me night watchman. He loved to enlighten me about myself in late-night conversations: 'Weissenstein, I've been thinking about you for a long time. You know what you are? A spice-box somebody spilled.' Well, what do you know!

I needed Fanta for that. If he'd at least explained to me his own fate and fortunes, but he only ever explained mine. Even that I could have lived with. But once, in my sleep, I knocked a bottle off a shelf, right above the sofa I slept on. The following morning, when Fanta woke me from a crippling stupor, there were dead mice, rats and a cat lying around a bittersweet smelling pool on the floor. There they lay, foe and friend. 'If I hadn't had something to do here this morning, you'd be lying there too,' said Fanta. The man had a heart.

"I lasted the longest at blind Kilian's place. He lived on the left bank of the river, in that old canal-like lane they call Little Venice, where a slender arm of the Moldau embraces Kampa Island. Kilian's dungeon-like room was ground level on the one side and just above water level on the other. Water sometimes got in during spring but that didn't bother Kilian, because all he had was an iron bed. I first met Kilian when his long white cane slipped out of his hand once and was just about to fall through a sewer grate and disappear into the depths. I caught the cane just in time and accompanied the blind man home. 'There's a petroleum lamp for guests,' he said, 'and an old straw mattress that's finally dry again. It's leaning up against the wall with the narrow end down. But first come here so I know how you look.' He ran his fingers over me, palpating my head, my features, my build. 'Poor fellow,' he said. He himself was a giant. We sat in the dark. I hadn't turned on the lamp, not wanting to act too important. 'The window is grated,' he said, 'it faces the water. A single leaf falls on its surface, I hear it. And here's a trapdoor in the floor. But don't mess around with it. You won't find any treasure behind it.' I came to his place a lot after that, always after dark, vanishing before sunrise. I didn't want to see more than he did. 'You're a fool,' he said, 'if you want to know what I know, you have to come in the daytime once. You're weaker than me. You need the daylight. You stumble. I don't.' And so sometimes I came in the daytime. It was a good enough place to spend the night. Things went on like this for some time. Only once, when I had a little money — I don't remember how I'd gotten it — I suggested paying something for my night's lodging. Kilian grew furious, swung his stick at me and hollered, 'If you want to pay then go to a hotel and never come back.' He didn't stop yelling till I really did leave, and I did in fact go to the Old Post Inn. The room there smelled like disinfectant, and above the bed hung a picture of the blind Jan Žižka dying under an oak tree, because, come what may, the Czechs are national-minded. Doors were being slammed all night and I slept like in the midst of a battle, but I had enough money to last me a week. Then I knocked at Kilian's door again. 'Aha,' he said and let me in.

"With Vlasta I could usually only spend the afternoon. Toward evening she maneuvered me out. How could a person keep their head above water leading a life like this? I can't exactly tell you. Certainly I'm guilty of a swindle or two myself. But what are these compared with my really serious transgressions. One time Vlasta found a bicycle in her attic. She imagined me as a telegraph boy or something. Women sometimes have the funniest ideas. Well, I had a better idea of how to earn money with the bike. I put a sign on it that read, 'By bike from

Lisbon to Vladivostok,' and went from table to table collecting money at beer gardens. It went well enough for one summer. My fellow Praguers understood me. The thought of distant lands enticed them. In late fall I pawned the bike. In the winter I sold the pawn ticket. I worked different jobs too. I suffered every fate, I waited on impatient customers, I slaved away in a boiler room, my face lit by the blazing fire, and working as a coolie I ate kitchen scraps and refuse."

"Weissenstein, you're spinning yarns. You got that from a Werfel poem."

"Surely, but I'm the one who made it come true. Looking back, it seems to me that I simply *was* the era with all its division and turmoil."

"Each one of us is the era, Weissenstein."

"But some of us are like collecting lenses, we condense the phenomena inside ourselves. Don't think I'm proud of it. There's nothing enviable about it. It's just plain sad. There's nothing sad about the ordinary life of an ordinary human being who's made of cork and always floats on the surface, a person who doesn't expect too much and isn't too fearful either. But enough of my musing and brooding. Let's get back to the facts.

"I saw how Vlasta struggled with Philomena, even though she had never met her. And my swearing I'd never so much as touched Philomena made the situation a thousand times worse, for it elevated Philomena into a sphere that was incomprehensible and unattainable for Vlasta. Nothing is more hateful than the incomprehensible and unattainable. Then again, the fact that I suffered from never having touched Philomena, and because I refused to do so I was all the more intimate with Vlasta, was something she couldn't fail to notice, and it only amplified her suffering immeasurably.

"'You mean she's chaste,' she sobbed, 'and immaculate, or so you think, and so she's the opposite of me. She's virtuous like a Madonna. Well, let me tell you why. Because you've got a pumpkin head, donkey ears, and a nose that points southwest. She'd do it with someone else, just not with you. Do you think I do it with you out of love? Očenášek and little Brandeis love me, so does that Hadrbolec from the National Theater and Hugatschek the coffeeman.' — 'Which Hugatschek the coffeeman?' I screamed. — 'How should I know? I only know his first name. He deals in coffee and smells like it too. He's better than you, believe me.' — I roared as if she'd kicked me in the heart. She was pleased by this, and began to soften her insults, merely calling me a lousy pug and her beloved freak, and granting me the most vehement amorous favors while continuing her mockery of me and declaring: 'Just don't go thinking this means anything. Aunt Hrdličková wipes the toilet seats in the lavatories at the Municipal House and munches on pears while she does it. That's what it means.'

"I learned to hate her, which failed to keep me away from her. I transformed myself into her and came to know her clients first-hand. I felt how I smelled like her powders, violet soap and disinfectant, felt like I had them on my own body, her pleated cambric blouses, tormented myself with the way she lured and the way she repelled as well as the way she yielded, shared her grievances, repudiated the whole of this lousy life, contemplated the cheapest methods of suicide, drowning, jumping from the window, hanging, slitting your wrists, the methods of the poor. And then, with unbridled arrogance, still as Vlasta, I began to take comfort in me, Weissenstein Karl, to long for me, to present myself to me with face flushed, to take on gigantic proportions, curls flowing freely, an archangel with its sword firmly drawn. And the more triumphal I imagined myself, the more I became aware of my horrid dwarfishness, my elephant ears, my incipient baldness, my misshapen skull, my whole wretched, miserable existence. Attacks like these usually came on Sundays. Sunday is the day of guilt and conscience. Those who can pray should pray, those who can sing should sing hymns, and when they're finished doing so should hasten to a soccer match, an outing, or the movies. Else he runs the risk of killing himself or someone else. Sunday is God's day of rest — and the devil's workshop.

"It was in this kind of mood that I ran to Aunt Karla one Sunday. Her fifth-floor courtyard apartment in an old building on Krakauergasse was decorated with theater memorabilia, mostly related to light opera and operetta, not because she herself had been in the theater but simply because she was fond of it and had been since her youth. Her appreciation of this art was formed early on by *Fatinitza*, *Die Fledermaus*, *La fille du régiment* and *The Gypsy Baron*, reaching its pinnacle after the turn of the century with *The Merry Widow*, *A Waltz Dream*, *The Divorcée* and *The Gay Hussars*. She was into serious theater, too, but her heart's content and her fervent humming was still reserved for 'You'll Find Me at Maxim's,' 'Every Woman is a

Riddle,' 'Music at Night Gives Me Thrills of Delight,' and the like.

"And so on Aunt Karla's walls or propped on her dresser and sundry étagères, in short wherever there was the least bit of space, she had photographs of soubrettes and comic actors, youthful heroes, buffos and prima donnas, some with personal dedications and autographs, even one that I really envied her for. I'm talking about her photo of Girardi. I never saw Girardi in person, but Herr Werfel, sitting at his café table, once did an impersonation, a Valentin number from *Spendthrift*, and claimed he was a man of genius. He died along with Old Austria. Girardi was a part of it. What use would successor states have been to him? His picture now hung on the wall at Aunt Karla's. The fact that she called him 'tip-top' was the highest compliment coming from her, who was otherwise so sparing with praise, and it lent her whole operetta ambiance a certain kind of dignity.

"'Good that you're here,' said my aunt, 'but have some coffee first, 'cause I'm afraid I have some bad news for you.' — I thought she might want to recoup some money I owed her. She did that sometimes, lovingly and despairingly, so I wasn't afraid of that. Once she even slipped me a letter: 'If you don't make an effort to pay me back I see no alternative but to take you to court. Loving kisses from your Aunt Karla.' And the next minute she'd say: 'Don't get all bent out of shape. I don't mean it badly.' So I wasn't exactly scared of her news. I sat down and drank my coffee and ate a crescent roll too. While my auntie sat there in pregnant silence, I grabbed a red-velvet photo album and studied the pictures in it: Angelo Neumann, the director with the giant handlebar mustache; Johanna Buska, Mizzi Zwerenz, Mizzi Zamara, Mizzi Jeritza and a host of other Mizzis.

"'Put away the album,' said my aunt, 'put the Carlsbad cup on the saucer. Your father died.'

"I didn't know how I was supposed to act upon hearing news like that. My father had vanished from my memory long ago. It didn't seem like I ever had one to begin with. Neither in my dealings with the literary men and their followers nor when I was in the military, nor in connection with Vlasta or Philomena, nor in any way at all while poetizing, loving, starving, swindling, slaving — in nothing, nothing at all, had my father made his presence felt ever since I'd run away from him. Except as the root cause of my existence, but even that was uncertain. I was ashamed of this afterthought the moment I had it, and consoled myself by the fact that I'd stolen it from the literati.

"'The funeral's the day after tomorrow,' said my aunt. 'I'll pay your fare.' I took the money, determined to take Philomena out to the 'Fidlovačka,' a Prague public festival she'd always wanted to go to. 'You're not inheriting anything,' my aunt explained reassuringly. 'Your father invested almost everything he had in war bonds, so it's good as gone. He lost the rest through speculation. Or so I've heard. But maybe your grandmother tucked some away for her Hugatschek. Supposedly there are back taxes, and three mortgages on the house.' — 'How do you know all this?' I asked, while fiddling with a photo of Hans Winckelmann as Siegfried. — 'Aunts just know,' she said, shrewdly. 'Don't worry too much about it. That's how things tend to end. But you should still go to the funeral.'

"So my father was suddenly back, even though he wasn't there at all. I was determined at first not to go, and to use the money on the Fidlovačka, not to mention Hungarian salami for Vlasta, a favorite of hers. But my determination crumbled overnight. It's nearly impossible to defy a dead person. The greatest surprises are always your own doing. Suddenly I was the son of my father. All my objections to him and his business, to the way he had treated me and to everything he stood for suddenly gave way. What remained was the thin yet indissoluble and inseparable thread of life from him to me, a life which may have been ugly, painful, damnable, disgraceful and full of guilt, but for all that was still astonishing, simply because it was. Was it possible that a father like that through a son like me could manifest the divine? What was one to think of Him who wasn't disconcerted by likenesses the likes of us?

"I took the train to Tschaslau, hiked to Potschaplitz and managed to make it to the funeral just in the nick of time. I didn't see my grandmother, of course, but I did see someone who was probably the much-lauded Hugatschek. He acted grief-stricken, was neatly dressed and surely much more dignified than me, which by the way was not saying much. I kept to the rear of the procession and tried not to give myself away. That wasn't too difficult, since many years had passed. Perhaps some people did recognize me, but if they did they didn't let on. A few of my father's old customers were there whose drinking days must have been over. While old Rabbi Flammerschein delivered his closing remarks, I overheard them discussing how their fields now belonged to the loan fund of St. Wenceslaus, which didn't know what to do with them though, which is why they kept on working the land as if nothing had ever happened. Simply not to bother, that was always the strongest weapon. '*Hatzur tamim po'alo*, The Rock! His work is perfect, praised be the Eternal One, the Righteous Judge who inflicts and heals all wounds.' There was a moment I felt impelled to step forward, but I sensed my unworthiness. I wouldn't have known how to recite the Orphan's Kaddish anyway. So I listened to the other's voice. 'Praised, glorified, exalted and extolled be the name of the Holy One, amen.' On account of this urge to step forward, when I felt it was up to me to say the prayer for the dead, do you think that because of that split-second urge I might be judged more leniently? Well, be that as it may, on the way back I endeavored to be grateful to my father. I tried to see some merit in him. I did my best to justify his weaknesses and not to gloss over my own. I wondered whether he'd done well to be my father, if he'd done himself a service. I pondered if I'd ever done something that pleased him, since that would have been a reason to be grateful. But I hadn't done anything that pleased him, and he hadn't done anything that pleased me either. True, what did I even know about him? No more than he knew about me. Perhaps he loved me in his own fashion. But he should have loved me my way. And I should have loved him his way. It was all a sham, all out of whack. Who had started it? Not me. That could be historically proven. But no matter what evidence I presented, he had the stronger advocate: Death.

"I had to change trains at Kolín. It was pouring rain. Suddenly, on the platform, I was standing across from Philomena and her mother. 'I just buried my father.' — 'We just visited an uncle who runs a tenant farm nearby.' The uncle was supposed to pick them up in his carriage but hadn't arrived yet. Philomena was delighted about our unexpected encounter. She was even trembling. Her mother was less delighted. How could she have thought highly of shabby, ugly me? Did she have any choice but to hope that her daughter might find someone better? But the fact I was coming from my father's funeral made her more lenient toward me. We waited and talked and I missed my train. 'I knew it was your train,' Philomena whispered later. I didn't care much about missed connections. It's always just coincidence anyway whenever you catch a train, and then there's still the question of whether or not you caught the right one. The answer might only come decades later, if it comes at all. So I'd missed that train, and the next one was leaving many hours later, at four o'clock in the morning. 'What bad luck,' lamented Philomena, but it didn't sound sincere. 'It's no trouble for me to wait,' I said, 'I'm just happy we met.'

"Finally her uncle arrived, an old-fashioned, massive, mustachioed Bohemian tenant farmer. He still used a horse and carriage even though the automobile age was well underway. The reason he was late, he said, was that Kaiserstrasse was paved with concrete and his landau got stuck in the mud on the detour he had to take. He still said 'Kaiserstrasse,' Emperor's Road, perhaps in deference to his horses. Philomena introduced me. 'And just imagine,' she said quickly, 'the poor fellow missed his train on account of us, just because he wanted to keep us company. Now he has to wait here till four in the morning.' — 'To make things worse, he's just come from his father's funeral,' her mother added, thinking nothing of it. But Philomena cut in at once: 'Yes, and at a dark and lonely train station in his frame of mind, my God.' — 'There's no such word as must,' her uncle cut her short, 'the gentleman can stay the night at our place and continue his journey in the morning.' It was a cordial-sounding invitation, one I eagerly accepted and which earned her uncle a kiss from Philomena. When we climbed into his landau he asked: 'Where's your luggage?' I had none. He frowned and merely said: 'What? No luggage?' — 'He's coming from his father's funeral,' Philomena reminded him. 'Aha,' said her uncle, but when we hit the road he added: 'Even then you have some luggage.'

"As we drove he showed us where his fields began, talked about sugar beets, wheat and potatoes, about the weather, the trouble with farmhands, who were nothing but a lazy pack of thieves, as well as his troubles with the tax officials, all of whom were scoundrels. His speech left the clear impression that only tenant farmers were decent people, however plagued by injustice and handicapped by fate they were. I was careful not to comment. The women held their tongues too. Philomena's uncle was a widower and childless. I noticed that my presence was perceived by Philomena's mother as being inappropriate and awkward. But it couldn't be helped now, and after three-quarters of an hour's journey we trundled into the yard of a two-story, rectangular building with stables on the ground floor and living and sleeping quarters above them.

“A maid in felt slippers served dinner. The portions were skimpy. ‘She used to work for the Blaus in Kostelec and thinks that’s fancy,’ said Philomena’s uncle disapprovingly. ‘There’s three times as much in the kitchen,’ said the maid in her defense. ‘Then take away what you brought us and bring in what’s left in the kitchen,’ ordered the uncle. He fetched a squat bottle of Melnik wine after dinner and began to talk about his relatives. He began by praising the overall character of every family member, one by one, dead or alive, then moved on to specifics and disparaged each one of them in such a way that you thought he was talking about a band of robbers. Then he sat down at the piano and performed with great feeling the familiar crowd-pleaser ‘The Dream of a Reservist.’ The two women applauded this childless widower, and I had no choice but to join them.

“After that the uncle and his maid escorted us to our quarters, the maid leading the way with a pair of burning candles in a candleholder, there being a partial blackout in the house — ‘it happens whenever there’s company,’ he snarled. Philomena and her mother each had a room in one wing, though not right next to each other, and I had one around the corner, albeit in the same hallway. In view of my lack of luggage, the uncle had left me a nightshirt on the bed. It was white and much wider and longer than me, the seams were trimmed with red-and-white embroidered fleur-de-lis, and I had to lift it up like a dancer whenever I took a step in it. In a wall mirror I caught my reflection, clad in a gathered shirt that made me look like a ballerina, and was suddenly terrified by the mysteries of the bourgeoisie.

I crawled into bed and heard the rustling trees in the yard. I don't know what kind of trees. Professor Bachrach always said that those who have a good grasp of nature can tell a tree by the rustling of its leaves. But who could ever learn a thing like that? The room itself was soon no longer silent. I began to hear the manifold sounds of matter, the articulation of its nightly struggle with the forms it's expected to assume. It probably does this all the time, but at night it's much more noticeable, at least to the attentive listener. Matter whispers 'too big,' 'too small,' 'misappropriated,' 'debased to the point of absurdity.' Forms demur: 'too dry,' 'too moist,' 'too smooth,' 'too rough,' 'too hard,' 'too soft,' 'what are we supposed to do with you?' If humans think they're the only ones burdened with cares and anxieties, they're mistaken. So even though I had stretched out in bed, I long suspected it wouldn't stay that way. The struggle of forms with matter proved contagious, the deep unrest of these objects imparted itself to me. I sensed that this night would be decisive, that either I myself would do something unexpected or something unexpected would happen to me. For why would Fate, or why would God, make such elaborate arrangements just to bring me here for a single night, to the holding of a lonely Bohemian tenant farmer together with his niece, the object of my desire? What made this night different from all the rest? Not for me to just leave the next morning, to the station at Kolín and from there back to Prague, tritely expressing my thanks for the hospitality and nightshirt, without the slightest thing having happened.

"So I listened to the night attentively and waited. I don't

even know anymore: Did I go to her or did she come to me? Who, when he's doing something, knows how much of it is actually his own doing and how much he simply endures? The rooms flowed into each other. I couldn't even say what kind of blissfulness I felt, if I entered Philomena or, being Philomena, received myself in her. In my memory this night sometimes seems incredibly brief, almost lightning-like, and sometimes endlessly long, full of power and weakness, comforts and horrors, full of the suspicion that even the most beloved individual is an endangered creature in our sinister hands, hands which the very next moment might fall prey to utter madness. It was a first and therefore last night. The second and third times are repeatable. The second and third of anything are relative to each other and can thus be exhausted by comparison. But the first and last are beyond comparison.

"Herwarth Walden once said to me: 'Weissenstein, what kind of Expressionist are you? Forget about the "like"! People nowadays don't say, "You're like a flower." They say, "You *are* a flower!" Show by declaring!'

"I would have preferred to sneak out of the house first thing in the morning, but I owed it to Philomena not to cause a commotion. At breakfast I asked about the earliest train, and when her uncle gave me to understand that he couldn't bring me to the station until the afternoon I declared right then and there that I'd walk it. 'It would take you two and a half hours,' said her uncle, 'and it's still raining.' 'All the same,' I answered, 'I have business to attend to.' 'What business can you possibly have,' remarked her uncle, 'you're running like you've got my silver spoons tucked in your boots.' 'But my Aunt Karla is seriously ill,' I lied. 'Well that's a different story. In that case I'll have the horses harnessed.' 'No,' I cried 'I want to walk,' and I ran off just like that, with a tumultuous 'adieu' for Philomena, out of the house and into the rain.

"I ran like a thief, the Eumenides hard on my heels. I ran down muddy paths, sometimes skirting fields, most of the time not even toward the station. Faster, faster, Weissenstein! That's life! Over hill and over dale, over ditch and over hedge. At times I rushed over clods of earth and stumbled into furrows in the pelting rain, I fought my way through thickets, waded through streams, crawled up a rocky hill, which was totally useless and which I only did to make things as hard as possible on me, to burden myself with punishment upon punishment, penance after penance. But all to no avail. I could hear Vlasta's laughter, giving me a run for my money. After many hours, sopping wet and caked with mud, I somehow made it to the station, just in time to catch the very train I had missed exactly twenty-four hours earlier on account of the conversation I was having on the platform with Philomena — though the real reason I missed it was to enable the total transformation of her life as well as mine."

"Weissenstein, our lives are transforming every single moment. We just don't notice it. Sometimes we merely deign to notice. And then we call it a fateful moment. But every moment is fateful."

"You're telling me! Only the clueless profit from life. But now I want to tell you something about the magical powers of lying. I lied about Aunt Karla being sick. But I lied the truth without even knowing it. For I headed straight from the station to her shop and when I got there it was closed. With a sense of foreboding I ran to her apartment. She was laid up in bed for real. 'Help me,' she groaned, 'I seem to be dying.' I reacted in the stupidest possible way. 'Why should you die? It says in the Bible: The days of our lives are threescore years and ten.' — 'The Bible also says that all flesh is like grass, it withereth and falleth away. I've got it on a plaque. Call Doctor Kral.'

"Since my aunt didn't have a telephone, I ran to the office of the aging physician. When I got there they told me he'd left and gone home. When I got to his apartment they told me he hadn't arrived yet. So I waited. After a while they told me he called and would be home later. When later? He was in a consultation at the clinic, they said. I ran to the general hospital and made my way to the clinic I had been directed to, a room that looked like the waiting room of some lonely station on the Trans-Siberian Railway. I haven't the faintest idea how those stations look in real life. Maybe they're cozy. Behind a table, reading a book, sat a cross between a nurse and a policewoman. From time to time she laughed. I thought of my aunt being all alone. Would death be all I had in life? 'I'm thirsty,' I said to the sexless person in charge. Without looking up from her book, she pointed to a carafe and a glass. It was old, stale water that had stood there for at least eight days. I drank it anyway, I even enjoyed it, for in me rages a childhood thirst, and when I drink, no matter what, I slake an ancient, unceasing thirst. 'The water's good,' I said, since I had the urge to speak. — 'The water is bad,' said the sexless person, 'and I want to read.' — 'What are you reading?' I asked. — '*The Wretched* by Hugo,' she laughed. — 'What's so funny about that?' — 'When you've been in this hospital for twenty years you can laugh about almost anything.' Finally old Doctor Kral appeared, with a gentleman known throughout Prague as Chief Clerk Neuern. 'So it couldn't be helped,' the latter said, 'life is made up of funerals.' He said it like a greeting, bowed and took his leave. Now I approached Doctor Kral and asked him to come with me straight away to see Aunt Karla. 'Who's Aunt Karla?' — 'She knows you,' I said, then filled him in. — 'So, she knows me. Can't it wait till tomorrow? I haven't even supped yet.' — 'She's dying,' I said, and, although I couldn't have known it, I said it with such conviction that good Doctor Kral went with me immediately and even paid for a cab. One look at me and he must have known it wouldn't be a lucrative case, but he belonged to that breed of doctors who practiced their profession in order to help, and not just to help themselves either.

"He regarded my aunt, did his examinations and then said what I'd realized myself as soon as we entered the room: 'She has indeed passed away. Half an hour ago. But even two hours ago there was nothing I could have done for her. A natural death, as they say.' He asked about her circumstances and next of kin. 'A son,' I said. 'But he's in a traveling theater, I don't know where. And an ex-husband. In America.' — 'America is big,' said Doctor Kral. 'The best thing would be to notify the authorities. I'll make out a death certificate.' He put on his coat and glanced at the walls. 'Well looky here, Klara Ziegler, and here's Sonnenthal. Those were the days.' Then Doctor Kral left.

"I was left alone with my aunt, who incidentally didn't look very corpselike at all but kind of cheerful lying there in her bed, as if the esteemed doctor's visit had done her a world of good. Doctor Kral may have shut her eyelids but her face had not lost much of its color, her fingers could relax now, she no longer had to tie bows and ribbons, gather veils, adjust buckles, fix artificial flowers and plumes, all the many things she did for the Sundays of market women and servant girls. Next to her bed, on an armchair, lay her purse. 'Open it,' said the slightly parted lips of my aunt. 'and take what you need.' — 'How can I,' I protested, 'that would be stealing.' — 'Don't be stupid. Take it before someone else does!' she ordered. Her helpfulness was truly unlimited. So I took. Not everything, but as much as I thought I needed. By God, a person's got to live. I thanked her and left.

"Hers was a pauper's funeral that not even the habitual beggars took the trouble to attend. Only the janitor's wife and two market women came, all of them in hats that were obviously the work of Aunt Karla and were thus their way of paying their last respects to her. A peculiar painter was there too, one who had known Aunt Karla and who made his living doing pastel portraits of the elderly, which he then, when they died, offered for sale to the relatives. 'You're one of the bereaved, aren't you?' he murmured to me. 'Yes, I am, perpetually,' I said. He unrolled a colored-pencil drawing of my aunt on brown packing paper. I bought it for almost all of the money I'd taken from her purse.

The facial features in the picture, inasmuch as they resembled my aunt's, seemed to be saying to me: 'You see how right you were to take the money?'

"The more thousandfold you're entangled, the lonelier you become. It sounds astonishing, but the more you lose, the more you have to lose. For the first time you really become aware of what remains in your possession, and even for the poorest it grows in importance. A time now lay ahead of me in which I'd forget more than ever that I was in fact a kind of poet. It began with my employment at the Masopust Bookshop. Back when I consorted with the living Expressionists, I counted myself among them and, indeed, I *was* them. But now I was mainly dealing with dead classical authors, and this took me away from literature. I came to Masopust through Vlasta. He came from the same region she did, and may have even been an occasional client of hers. I didn't pursue the matter. After Aunt Karla's funeral she loaded me with reproaches at first, on account of my prolonged absence, but then she was moved to tears when I told her about the two deaths, before she finally said: 'You're hiding something from me, you rascal, I'm waiting for the third corpse.' But she couldn't get anything out of me. 'I'm respectable,' she said, before she began to tell me that Masopust was looking for a shop assistant. Then she began to describe for me the blessings of an ordered life and steady income. Finally she embraced me and sighed: 'I'm respectable, 'cause I work against my own best interests.'

"At the time I didn't really understand her, but I went to Masopust anyway. His shop was on Hibernergasse. His bushy blond head of curls marked him as a bookseller with ideals. He knew about me already, and showed me with the minimum of words my place as well as my tasks. The bookshop was Czech but had an extensive section of used books in German, and it was here that Masopust thought I'd be useful. I was supposed to keep them in order and catalog them. In particular, I was expected to know what we had in stock, along with taking care of mail orders and running errands. Masopust bought up the libraries of former Austrian aristocrats whose estates were liquidated after the collapse of the empire. They contained some quite curious and rather rare publications. I marveled at all the things that had been printed and evidently read, too, over the course of the centuries. Some editions had the coat of arms of their erstwhile owners embossed on the covers but had never actually been opened. The gilt-edged pages were still stuck together, unmarred by a single mildew stain. Other volumes had clearly been read and reread from generation to generation, the names and dates of their readers having been inscribed on the flyleaves. I could more or less chart the shifting interests of the Kolowrats, Zedtwitzs, Sternbergs, and other noble families. Sometimes I was moved by the ruined aristocracy.

"The stockroom was a dark, elongated cellar, poorly lit by a few electric bulbs and a little window that gave onto Hibernergasse, though you didn't actually see the street, you only saw the cobblestones and the feet, pant legs or skirts of passersby, whose bodies, not to mention their heads, were all but invisible. My desk, with my catalogs, card indexes and registers, was located underneath the window and led a veritable life of its own, a fascinating world of order that was utterly new to me, the alphabetized existence of poets, writers, scholars, experts, print runs, publishing houses, prices, listings — a world in which the contents themselves had actually lost their meaning. Bestsellers, rare editions, reduced items and plenty of schlock — that was the social structure prevailing in this world of books. From my desk I occasionally looked up and through the window at the relentless stream of human extremities passing by outside, between which once in a while a dog, a sparrow, a pigeon or a cat would appear in its entirety. Doctor Fanta had once told me about Plato's outlandish cave, and the men in chains inside it who could only glimpse the shadows of existence, which they took for actual reality. That's basically how I felt in Masopust's storeroom. What's more, the little cellar window was glazed, the glass cloudy and grimy, and in front of it was a grate. It's incredible all the things that life still offers to observant eyes even with all of that in between. Of course inside, too, I encountered all manner of things incomplete: second, third or fifth volumes, old Bibles without the title page, bindings without the spine, almanacs missing their copper engravings. 'What do you want,' said Masopust, 'it's the same with people. Besides, everything finds a taker sooner or later.' It sounded like he was referring to me.

"But the books soon had such power over me that I not only ordered and cataloged but also began to read them. I read everything, from Abraham a Sancta Clara to Zschokke. And that's when I realized that poets can prevent you, perhaps even *should* prevent you, from writing anything yourself. After all, creating means lighting your own fire and not lighting up from others, means hewing from stone or working with wood, extracting it for better or for worse and letting it shine, or — as only the greatest can do — reaching for the stars and bringing them down to earth. But most of those who write know nothing of stone or wood, of better or worse, let alone stars. And so it was books that kept me from literature. And good thing, too.

"So now that I was earning a modest income, I rented an attic room next to the 'Old Ungelt,' I owned more than two shirts, I got my wardrobe secondhand from 'Jakob Rothberger Heirs,' indeed in my own way I'd become a real Rastignac, loved by two girls at once. I was sure, though, that the whole thing couldn't last, was secure in my insecurity, insecure in my security. And when, coming from Vlasta or Philomena, I was alone in my attic room at night, with a view of the side entrance of Týn Church, I was suddenly overcome with anxiety. Anxieties are the diversion of the lonely. They appear in ever-new guises, filling every nook and cranny of the soul. As awful as they may be, what would we do without them, assuring as they do that we're always busy, that we always see ourselves as separate from the world and calculate its countless dangers?

"I only saw Vlasta on Sundays during the daytime now, or whenever during the week I could steal an hour in the afternoon or contrive to run an extra errand for Masopust. She seemed content enough with this set-up, for that was the price of my bourgeois existence which she herself had arranged for me. She thought of me as a dress-up doll with a costume sewn by a little girl. She knew, of course, that I kept the embers burning with

Philomena, but consoled herself with the notion that I only ever saw her on rare occasions, and surely never at night. Vlasta, moreover, was laboring under the misconception that she'd done me yet another good turn. She made the same mistake that many women do of assuming you can win a man's heart — if I might, for a moment, call myself a man — by hard work, sacrifice and sheer ability. She got this impulse from a world she didn't belong to but probably would have liked to. At least that's how I saw her. That was her awful lot in life. Women seem the strongest when their motives are obscure.

"Just don't think that in telling these things it's always me I've got in mind. I probably stand for many people. Otherwise my story wouldn't be worth the telling. It's impossible that God intended me as an isolated case. And I never claimed that I was. I'm not saying I'm the most unworthy of all. That would be presumptuous. But I'm surely one of the least. This must be a very big group of people, the least of this world. A veritable army. Many, many armies. Of various degrees and ranks. There are those who know they're among the least, those who don't and therefore think they're something better, and those who know but refuse to believe it.

"I did an experiment to see what connects people regardless of their rank. I interviewed the 'chair lady' at the Municipal Park, the female impersonator Vlaštovka at the White Swan cabaret, and Alexander Moissi, the actor, to find out what they have in common. Don't be surprised that I met Herr Moissi. I knew Herr Werfel and Herr Kafka too, Herr Brod and Herr Willy Haas, and I even knew you, though the lot of you barely knew me. You remember the 'chair lady' at the Municipal Park, with her pince-nez on a black ribbon, the black leather bag slung around her shoulder and the ticket-puncher on her belt. She worked for City Hall, selling pink tickets for four hellers a piece that entitled you to sit for an hour on one of the iron chairs in the park, which were city property and rather uncomfortable. The tickets were covered with numbers, a kabbalah of twelve months, twenty-eight to thirty-one days of the month, seven days of the week and twenty-four hours a day. The entire concept of time was captured on that little pink slip of paper, and no one could escape it. The back of the ticket, alongside an advertisement for the Zátka soda-water company, threatened certain punishment for those who unlawfully parked their behinds on any of these municipal chairs. The chair lady, like one of the Fates, relentlessly used her puncher to mark the month and day and hour. She was getting up in years, always dressed in black, and I even knew her in person, since every spring she came to Aunt Karla to have her black taffeta hat remodeled, for the woman had her dignity and wore the hat now with the brim turned up, now with the brim turned down, sometimes with a stiff corded ribbon, sometimes with a velvet bow. She took in less money than the weekly allowance the municipal government paid her, which for its part only retained this peculiar, completely superfluous position out of deference to tradition and to keep a penniless person employed. She was often the victim of malicious fraud, since many a person sat down without paying only to take to their heels as soon as they saw her coming. One time I asked her a question, about the easiest and the hardest thing in her life. I didn't ask out of the blue, but had a number of preparatory talks with her first, during which I had heard a lot of sad things about her past and present. The easiest thing, she told me, was life itself, despite all the poverty, hardship and deprivation. The hardest thing, though, was loneliness. Loneliness, it turned out, was a constant companion, everything else was just temporary. But loneliness got harder from one day to the next.

"I met the female impersonator in the beer garden of the cabaret on Na Poříčí. He was married with two little children. His wife weighed two-hundred and ninety pounds and wore red-and-white striped stockings. No lack of national vigor there. His apartment was located in the suburb of Lieben and there wasn't a moment of peace there, for his wife's sister lived with them too, and the two women constantly chattered and cooked. 'From morning till night, our place is as loud as a shooting gallery. Our bed is a real switchyard, what with the children sleeping there too. I can imitate women in all walks of life. I even sing coloratura.' — 'What's the easiest and what's the hardest thing for you?' — 'The easiest thing,' said Vlaštovka, 'I'm not too sure about that. Nothing is easy. The hardest thing, though, is loneliness.'

"Surely hearing about Herr Moissi is what interests you the most. It's surprising enough that such a big star would open up to a nobody like me. It was after a performance of *The Living Corpse*. The audience was still applauding at the end and I'd left my standing-room spot and headed to the stage door in the hope of getting one more glimpse of the great man before he left the theater. I wasn't the only one waiting there, but it took a long time, and finally, after about an hour, I was the last one remaining. I assumed that Moissi had left the theater, perhaps through an exit unknown to me, and was about to leave myself when, just to be on the safe side, I asked Podlesný, the doorman, one more time, who answered that Moissi had left already, had slipped right past me half an hour ago.

"'Which Moissi has left already?' a voice rang out from nowhere. 'Has he really? Have you waited for nothing? Oh, how I feel for you!' He eyed me attentively. 'But seriously, my friend. What did you want to tell me?' I didn't really *want* to tell him anything. After a brief interval of silence he said: 'You probably wanted to congratulate or thank me, or just have a so-called brush with fame. Fame, my young friend, is an orchestral fantasy and a much misunderstood topic. I'll make you a proposition. If you haven't got anything better to do, come along with me.' The invitation seemed inconceivable to me. After such a stellar performance, did he really have no better company than me? But, what do you know, the two of us walked alone through dark alleys until we got to the Blue Star Hotel. He could see I felt awkward at a place like this, so he ordered for me. I didn't know what I was eating, I was in such a trance that I might have easily mistaken a raw potato for pineapple. 'Now you see,' said Moissi, 'how reality looks. You see I'm no less lonely than the hurdy-gurdy man in the courtyard who gets tossed a ball of paper with a kreutzer wrapped inside. Everyone is also the opposite of themselves. You have to learn to transform yourself if you don't want to be hopelessly lonely.

The reason I became an actor was the thousand transformations it offered. The lines of the play are nothing but the words set to my transformations. The performer on stage, the audience member, those are always two forms of loneliness pitted against each other, like David playing the harp for Saul. And Saul dries the heavy tears that cling to the folds of the curtain. But what does David play? The Bible leaves it chiaroscuro. David plays his loneliness. Someday he'll cry, "Absalom, my son!"' Moissi paused for a while, then continued in a low voice: 'You know, I love the Russians. I've got some Russian roots, German and Italian too, even Albanian. But I like playing Tolstoy best. There's a Russian theater company called "The Blue Bird." They play a short, silent scene from *The Queen of Spades*. Very simple: just a young girl at a dinner party standing off to the side, looking out a window and drying a tear. You don't see what she's looking at. You don't see what she's not looking at. The whole thing lasts but a minute.' Moissi raised his napkin to his eye. Then he ascended the hotel stairs, utterly forlorn. Each step was singular. None seemed to have any connection to the other. He was not long for this world.

"Why, after all of that, should I talk about how hard my nights are? I continued going on walks with Philomena through the many gardens of Prague and occasionally on the usual outings to villages along the Moldau. Since that night at her uncle's farmstead I was very self-conscious around her, whereas she became more outgoing. I seemed to detect her becoming more beautiful from one moment to the next, but this just made me even more bashful. Her dark eyes had acquired an eager sparkle, her hair reflected metallic splendor, her temples and hands revealed shimmering transparencies — in short, everything about her was radiant with life, with the irrefutable proof of nature. I say nature because this might explain why the perfect and beautiful so often join forces with the inferior and unworthy. She asked me endless questions about my adventurous youthful wanderings, my heroic deeds in the military, my fame among the poets. I tried to portray all of this in its total nullity, but she took it for false modesty. I only wanted — so she objected — to hide my light under a bushel. How gutsy, gifted and generous I really was! I could have just as well laid it on thick for her and told her bare-faced lies about myself. She always seemed to be hoping that at some secluded place beyond the suburbs of Prague I would step out of the spotlight that she herself was shining on me, press her close to me, and add to my many victories the triumph of another embrace. For the first act of surrender wants to be redeemed an entire lifetime, hundreds and thousands of times. But the more Philomena sparkled, the more I retreated fearfully, avoided secluded places, took care not even to brush against her, much less to touch her, and when in innocent sincerity she put her arm through mine, when she placed her hand on top of mine, it felt like an iron weight to me and I looked for a suitable pretext to extricate myself. Of course she noticed, but among the many stratagems a person in love will use to help explain the disagreeable, truth is the last resort. It goes without saying that our meetings couldn't have been more innocent, and it also goes without saying that in Vlasta's interests — and my own, too — my behavior couldn't have been more false.

"We seldom stop to consider that an intrinsically unworthy person exhibits, on top of it all, the entire gamut of human failings that even the worthiest cannot elude. But the especially treacherous thing about fate is that these failings, which the worthy know well enough how to deal with, drag the unworthy into an abyss against which he is defenseless. That was what happened to me with my vanity. I felt ugly and old. Now, as the years go by, I know that back then I was still fairly young. But at the time I didn't really notice, or didn't dare acknowledge it. I seemed old to myself ever since I was a child, then later felt old among the poets, old among soldiers, old when I was with Vlasta, and old next to Philomena. The lonely individual is old, the guilty one is old. Have a bit of patience with me. I'm not just thinking of myself. Perhaps my story will be of use to others in their struggle against life's reprieves. That's why almost everyone, anyone I've ever met, gets their due in my telling. Human destiny is not so filtered that it plays out between a mere three or four characters, like in an old-fashioned novel. Entire worlds are exploding all around us constantly. I tell it as it was, I don't tamper. I don't speak just to pour my heart out, but because the dead, whose ranks back then I would very soon be joining, can convey some useful information to the living. You shouldn't be surprised if my advice sounds so emphatic at times. Only cynics conceal their warnings in subordinate clauses or parentheses. Those who care about others allow themselves to get riled up. Philomena had given me a cravat as a present — a 'necktie,' as they call it in Germany. But I'm an Austrian revenant, after all. Philomena had no real reason to give me this present, which she'd sewn herself on her mother's machine. The cravat was very long and wide, made of heavy, sturdy silk, claret-red with green polka dots worked into it. It was really quite fancy, in blatant contrast to the rest of my wardrobe. Even Herr Feldscharek, the engineer, could have cut a fine figure in it on his strolls along the Graben. I was no expert in tying a cravat. This one I carefully looped into the widest knot possible to show the material to its best advantage. But, tying it in front of the mirror, it really should have dawned on me that a clown like me can't dress up with impunity. I noticed how my face became distorted all of a sudden, how it pulled to one side and screwed itself up, the other side seeming to disappear completely, all the more so since my nose was pointing in that direction already. The face in the mirror was dreadful, but maybe I'd always looked that way and I just perceived it more clearly now on account of the cravat, which demanded something in return, some kind of expiation. Nothing in this world, no matter what it is, comes without atonement! But I didn't heed the warning. 'That's just the way I am,' I moped. The cravat put me in a devil-may-care kind of mood. After all, Philomena basically had me by the neck in the form of her cravat, and I carried this hold around my neck for all the world to see.

"It was surely a human but no less inexcusable weakness that the first time I wore the cravat was for Vlasta. I've always endeavored to locate my weaknesses, to talk to them and understand them. Each time, though, I end up falling victim to yet a new weakness that I haven't wised up to yet. Their number is legion. All the same, as soon as I got to Vlasta's she asked: 'Where'd you get the tie?' Now, most people in my position would have probably lied automatically. They would have said they got the cravat at a clearance sale or as a gift from Herr Pollak, the bank clerk, who incidentally did indeed pass on the occasional cravat to me that he found too grotesque. His girlfriend, Wanda, nearly left him once because of it. So I could have made do with the momentary advantage of a simple falsehood, whose role in day-to-day dealings is greater than the truth anyway. But I suddenly felt I'd come to Vlasta to make a point, to precipitate a decision, to set an avalanche in motion. Avalanches aren't caused by mistakes, and calamities are not the result of missteps. Rather, mistakes and missteps are the means that avalanches and calamities use. And so I told Vlasta the truth. For I'd come to bear witness to the truth. Lying would not have done me much good in the long run anyway. It would have merely been a dilatory tactic, and Vlasta's keen instincts would have ferreted out the truth before long. Simple natures are harder to deceive than sharp-witted intellectuals. I have my experience.

"Now, I would have considered myself happy if only she'd started to scream and curse. Instead she was silent. She sat down at a small dressing table and simply closed her eyes. It means a lot when a creature like Vlasta closes her eyes in front of a mirror. I would have been happy if only she had cried. But she didn't. Her countenance hung tearless and fixed in the mirror. Pale and remarkably narrow. Maybe it was a shoddy mirror that sucked out her color and distorted her proportions. But I only had a second to think about it, and the thought was refuted by what followed. Vlasta had always been well-proportioned and ruddy-complexioned. Now, in the mirror, she was haggard and pale.

"Those who don't love unconditionally, without reserve, always do the dumbest thing in situations like this. I stepped up behind her and asked, as it were, apologetically: 'Mousy's seedy?' There's little point inquiring into the etymology of this expression, for it's part of the private idiom, the dopey vocabulary of teasing and flirting that develops between couples over time. In our case it basically meant: 'You're not offended now, are you?' I would have been happy if she'd merely been offended. She didn't respond, her eyes remained closed. I put my hand on her shoulder. Then she opened her eyes. I would have been happy if she'd left them closed. It felt like the very first time I'd looked at a pair of eyes. Again I said something ridiculous, hoping it would incite her to load me with reproaches and release me from my torment. Still she remained silent. Then she grinned in the mirror. And I knew she wasn't grinning at me.

"Grinning, she rose to her feet and started to undress. Not a word was said. She was naked. Her gaze no longer sought me out, and I was unable to catch it. It wasn't that she was looking to the side or away from me. She looked at me without seeing me, and when I tried to capture her gaze her eyes became pupilless, like those of a stone goddess. The grin, however, stayed in place. Why didn't I run away then and there? Why do humans behave so inhumanely? Why did I do what everyone does?

She'd turned out the light. But I knew she was grinning. Why did I have no mercy? She chose to grin and bear it in silence until the bitter end. I gathered my clothes in the dark. I didn't find the cravat. I didn't bother looking, and left.

"When you're wound up, at your wits' end, and don't know which way to go, an old nocturnal city is like a wild forest. Buildings weigh heavily, corners wrench you around, you run in circles, blind alleys choke you, over the portal to the Platteis Passage sits an owl no one has noticed before. Horned owls hoot from ledges, foxes bark from cavernous portals. I hastened through covered passageways, zigzagged senselessly through Old Town, fled through the Ungelt courtyard, where — as usual — a dispute was being slugged out, ducked under the arches of St. Agnes Cloister, I ran and searched and didn't know why. I didn't know what I looking for, and yet I would find it. Even Vlasta's rectangular window cropped up before me again, its silhouette cast against the curtain. My hand was about to open the door. But then it went slack and I plodded on. I was well into Langengasse when I heard blind Kilian's cane tapping behind me.

"'I know the sound of your footsteps,' he said. 'Silence!' he ordered, 'You're coming from some misfortune.'

"'That's nothing special. I'm always coming from some misfortune.'

"'And you're heading for one too. Silence! Talking about it won't help at all. Take comfort: Every life is a failure.'

"His bald white head reflected the streetlights, and his long coat with oversized, pompon-like buttons made him look like a Pierrot. From a window came the shrill sound of a flute doing scales. 'Oho, you haven't learned humility yet,' he started up again. 'Are you still suffering from guilt? You'd like to be completely innocent, eh? You'd like to tyrannize others, each of whom is surely guilty. I've got a better idea. Come to my place. My trapdoor leads straight to the canal. You can make it look like an accident. I'll just slide the bolt back for you, and when I'm not paying attention or sleeping, you step on the grate and it's all taken care of. From Little Venice you'll be washed into the Moldau; from there, if you're lucky, to the Elbe, then on to the sea. Of course there are dams and locks in between, and some busybody might fish you out. Still, what do you think?'

"'It won't do me any good,' I said.

"'You see! Go on living the way you are. Certain kinds of fools are always in demand. Besides, guilt is best atoned for by simply staying alive. Human beings are condemned just by virtue of being human. Most people fail to understand that. It's a necessary circle. Come to my place. Maybe you'll get some sleep. Sleep puts a lid on evil, and even blots out scorn. If you don't sleep, though, which is probably more likely, and if you don't decide to atone by living, you can always open the trapdoor yourself. I don't even need to know, so you won't cause me any trouble. I wouldn't even have to lie. "Yep, he was here," I would say, "and fell in. Is there anything else I can help you with?"'

"'How did you recognize me by my footsteps? Thousands of people pass by here.'

"'And I recognize every one of them. I'm Argus-eared. The

Chodounský detective agency sometimes pays me to track people down. Their company sign has a piercing eye on it. And still they need me, the blind man. I can hear what they don't see. If it's someone I know, I can tell from their walk what's ailing them. You're coming from misfortune.' We crossed the bridge and passed the Institute for the Blind. 'They wanted to stick me in there. But I have to hear my cane tapping and people's footsteps. I'm too important. I make people more charitable and do them little favors. And if I were in there, I wouldn't have run into you just now. But you need some place to go. 'Cause you're headed for misfortune.'

"'I have my own room now.'

"'Not for a night like this.' We'd reached his dwelling. 'Lie down. Don't bother with the light. It's enough to listen and touch.' I heard the quiet murmur of the water nearby and all around me a colony of rats going about its business.

"'A woman once went to bed with me,' began Kilian after a while. 'It was dreadful. She thought she was being nice to me. You should have a taste of it too, she said. Does everyone do it like that? I asked. Everybody, no difference, she laughed, as if it were a gift. But I noticed she was lying. Nothing gives a person away like false laughter. I felt her face. You're cockeyed, I said, and you're ugly too. No one wants to do it with you. She howled: You eyeless monster! And I hollered right back: No, even I don't want you! Finally she left. Not that I didn't feel sorry for her. She'd thought she'd found a way out. I could have helped *her*, and not the other way around. Whichever way she died, and even if she's still alive, it was me who killed her.'

"Something prickly brushed against my arm and I started. 'Don't be alarmed. It's only Stutzel, my hedgehog. He eats the vermin.' — 'Why do you call him Stutzel?' — 'That's from my childhood. Back when I was six, and could still vaguely make things out, there was a neighbor woman with a short haircut. They called her Stutzel — "butch." She also wore wide, baggy trousers and rode a bicycle. People considered her dangerous. Once she leaned over to me, waved her hands in front of my eyes and said: Ha-ha, your auntie! At that very instant my eyesight was gone for good. Isn't that ridiculous? Stutzel, the woman with the hedgehog hair, was the last thing I saw in this world. After that I didn't see anything. At first she didn't notice I'd gone completely blind, and she kept on waving her hands in front of me. "Ha-ha, look at your auntie." I can still clearly see her spiky hair before me. I've had to use my ears and fingers to cobble together the rest of the world. I suppose the last thing you see with your eyes — even when you're dying — usually isn't worth much. And, anyway, why should it be more awe-inspiring than what you normally see? But I see your mind is wandering.'

"I was thinking of Vlasta. I knew she was not alone during most of the night, that she couldn't talk to herself. I felt the tremendous confusion that everyone caused in her. She'd appointed me as her steward, wanted me, the most confused of confusers, to create some order in her life. Why? Probably because I was so revoltingly ugly, which I'd never really noticed before until I was tying the cravat. She counted on me, like the woman who went to bed with Kilian just because he was blind.

But I was not reliable either. I'd failed her. I was much, much worse than the others who came to her. I took it for free. With what right? Why didn't she seek what everyone seeks, love what everyone loves, condescending to me instead in order to degrade me? I didn't think of Philomena, who didn't make me feel this way. I pulled myself together in the morning and, without even eating breakfast, went to Masopust's bookshop. There was much to be done. 'December is a strange month,' said Masopust, 'first it seems so far away, then it suddenly closes in and tears the old year down.' Why the secondhand section was also affected by the Christmas rush is one of the mysteries of business life. You don't, after all, give a dog-eared Plato as a present to someone, or Voltaire without a spine. And yet more used Reclam paperbacks were purchased in December than they were in November or January. All day long I made up packages, wrote up invoices, organized shelves and carried out bundles of paper. When I got back from the last of my errands, two gentlemen were standing in the shop who, by the look of it, weren't there to buy books.

"'There he is,' said Masopust, and his tone was a mixture of displeasure and suspicion. 'And right before Christmas,' he added reproachfully, as if somehow the way of the world were my doing, and the Gregorian calendar too. Masopust was pale. With the courtesy shown a man before his inevitable death sentence, a man who has not yet been convicted but whose guilt is beyond question, the two men asked me to accompany them to police headquarters. Walking down the Graben, they debated who makes the best knockwurst in Prague, a frequent point of contention in this city, capable of dividing families into opposing camps, much like the Montagues and Capulets. On Obstgasse it became too much for me and I blurted out, 'Koula.' It dropped like a bomb. 'Nailed it,' said the one detective. The other one gave up the fight. 'You might amount to something yet,' he said. They both patted me on the back. It seemed like I'd made some friends after all. But I still had to empty my pockets at the station. 'Routine procedure,' said one of the detectives reassuringly. Then they took me to a big room and made me wait there. On the benches along the walls sat individuals, male and female, most of whom behaved as if their being there was the greatest blunder in the history of officialdom at least since the arrest of Socrates, while others displayed a sympathetic indifference, as if to say: 'Don't expect more from an ox than beef.' Very few seemed to be truly troubled, and only one or two stared straight ahead in sheer desperation. In one corner of the room, with his back to a high window, which just to be on the safe side had bars, sat a uniformed policeman behind a desk whose only job, it seemed, was to keep tabs on everyone in the room and cross off from a list the names of the individuals who were called into other rooms for questioning. One of the persons waiting approached him. 'I'm here. Why is no one attending to me?' 'They'll attend to you more than you bargained for,' said the policeman. 'This is preposterous,' the man finally said to me, 'I tell old Pošusta: Lend me a hundred crowns. He says: But you have to give it back, and you'll never have that much. So I say: What do you mean, give it back? I said lend! And I reach into his cash-box. Just then a policeman comes — he must have been standing there waiting outside — and drags me away. Tell me, seriously: I never even saw or touched the money, and can't a person ask for a loan these days?'

"I couldn't answer that question. I didn't even know why I was there. I was guilty, sure enough. But this was a place where guilt played no role; lawful or unlawful, that's all they cared about here. It was not enough, of course, that you hadn't broken any laws. You had to be able to prove it. Providing proof, though, is the hardest thing in the world. And what would I have to prove? And whatever it happened to be, would I even want to prove it? They summoned me after about an hour. An official in a prison-like room ordered me to be seated. Then, for a while, he paced to and fro as if he were a prisoner himself, observing me while he did so, without so much as saying a word. Then, like an ambush, he suddenly held up my claret-red cravat. It was twisted-up and torn in one spot. 'Familiar with this?' he asked in a menacing voice. 'Yes,' I heard myself say, before a soft darkness enveloped me.

"When I came to, I was lying in my room and Masopust was sitting at my bedside. 'Of course I knew all along you were innocent,' he said. 'Here's some black coffee and rum. And here's ten crowns advance pay. What else can I do? You do what you can. Report back to work once you're all there. Now, during Advent, a person can't afford to be sick. Why are you looking around like that? What are you looking for?' — 'Where's my cravat?' — 'Cravat? What do you need a cravat for now? Oh, you mean *the* cravat. Corpus delicti, my friend.

It's torn anyway. The poor girl fell from the crossbars in the window. Unfortunately too late. She'd passed to the other side a few hours before. They suspected at first that someone had used the cravat to . . . Well, until the police physicians were able to determine irrefutably that she herself . . . Poor girl. I knew her. I know her neighborhood.' — 'But how did they know the cravat was mine?' — 'You've got a point there! How did they know? Truth will out. A certain Herr Brandeis provided the information. He told her on his way out: One of your customers forgot his tie. To which she answered: That was no customer, that was my Weissenstein Karl. They'd questioned at least a dozen people since the morning regarding the cravat. They had some names and descriptions from the girlfriend who found her in the morning.' — 'She must have given my name too.' — 'No, she didn't. It was Brandeis who tipped them off.' 'And she — I mean Vlasta — really said *my* Weissenstein?' — 'Yes. Exactly. I've got it straight from the report. The inspector is a friend of mine. If it really matters so much to you, Brandeis will corroborate it. I made some inquiries with the inspector. I wanted to know exactly the extent of your involvement. But there are no charges against you. I mean, everyone goes to a dame like that at some point or another.'

"'I'm not as innocent as you think.'

"'What? Hooey. You're a little overwrought, that's all, and it's made you get some funny notions in your head. The facts are unassailable.'

"'But you see what a danger I am to the world.'

"'You, a danger? Maybe the world is a danger to you. You suffer from a few delusions of grandeur, but not enough.'

"'I murdered her indirectly. Is that not enough?'

"'No, it's not. Not at all. You just feel important because of your cravat. Dead is dead. The important thing now is for the living to find some relief. Don't preoccupy yourself with death. That's for philosophers to figure out. The living should preoccupy themselves with life. Who's that on the wall over there?'

"'My Aunt Karla.'

"'You see, you've even got an aunt.'

"'She's dead.'

"'Well, there you go. Put it in a frame then.' And with that, he left.

"The funeral took place without a priest. There are no ceremonies for deaths like that. Still, it had a certain solemnity about it. There was black crepe and silver decorations. 'Herr Hugo paid for it,' Fanynka whispered. 'Which Hugo? Where is he?' — 'Don't shout like that! What's gotten into you? You expect him to come to the funeral too? The flowers are mine.' Even the janitor's wife came. 'She came to cry,' explained Fanynka. 'Now she's met her Maker,' said the janitor's wife, sobbing. I looked for myrtles at the florist. In vain. How inept and useless I am! In the end I had to settle for dahlias. Then I watched as a mound was formed from the layers of soil displaced from the ground to make room for the coffin. Maybe Kilian was right after all: it's presumptuous to feel too guilty. Guilt has a life of its own that is inaccessible to reason. Why was I actually so firmly convinced that what Vlasta couldn't bear was not being loved exclusively or sufficiently, even by a nothing like me, even though she'd surrendered herself to him? Maybe she sensed that her attack on Philomena had turned back against herself. And the fact that she said 'my Weissenstein Karl' was not so extraordinary after all. Indeed, she used to say 'my garbage can' too. Of course it depended on *how* she said it. Could little Brandeis reproduce the tone she said it in? Vlasta's intimate way of speaking, from the larynx of little Brandeis? That she used the cravat to carry out her plans was not necessarily symbolic either. Masopust was probably right again. She grabbed what happened to be at hand. Were there even plans? It might have been a state of mental confusion, embitterment over her derailed and bungled life, in which I myself had merely played one of the many supporting roles, perhaps the least of them. Maybe she was suddenly overcome by tremendous loneliness, the kind that separates human beings from humanity, from things, from everything that was and is, a state they call death and which she, by means of this act, was merely reaffirming. Love? What did I know about the way women love? She was accustomed to offering, with every possible nuance, an illusion of the most palpable way in which love is usually proven. But all this, of course, was nothing but empty and ignominious speculation, a pathetic attempt to shirk responsibility. For it was clear she'd suffered on my account, had given herself to me, opened her heart and confided in me.

"On the way back from Malvazinky Cemetery, Fanynka, who had stuck it out with me to the end, began to talk in a peculiar way. It was Hugo Kulík, then, who had paid for the funeral. Aha, so a completely different Hugo than the one I'd feared. Not Hugatschek, the terror-child of my grandmother. Kulík, Fanynka gave me to understand, had gone with Vlasta back in the day. She said 'with her' and not 'to her.' In Czech, too, as you well know, to go with somebody means a real relationship, a 'serious acquaintance.' But some time ago, long before I came along, Kulík got married. That kind of thing happens. And it's always a source of unhappiness. Later, once Vlasta started earning, he began to visit her again. Understandably enough. He started coming more and more often. And Vlasta used to say, 'Why shouldn't he?' We don't really know, of course, if she really took it so lightly. The men always figured the girls either felt nothing or only felt something with them. But that's not the way it is. Vlasta had always held Kulík in her arms 'with feeling.' 'Our type can only afford that with someone we really care about.' Now Kulík was planning to move. Where to? Away from Prague. As long as it's somewhere else. Leaving Prague basically meant saying goodbye to the world. And even if it was just to Pilsen, that was practically as far as Casablanca. 'I mean, he could have just as well joined the Foreign Legion.' So the fact that Vlasta used my cravat . . . that was no reason to flatter myself. If she'd had some hemp rope, or even Očenášek's suspenders, she would have done it with that, wouldn't she. And the dealer who sold her the rope surely wouldn't have seen himself as the cause of Vlasta's despair.

"Everything Fanynka told me on the way through Smíchov, and even when we stopped for hot dogs at the butcher's

— because it's in the nature of people to eat, even when they're coming from or heading toward death — all of these disclosures seemed intended to drive the point home that I didn't mean as much to Vlasta as I imagined, and, indeed, precisely that drove me to distraction all over again when I got back to my attic room. Fanynka was kindhearted, and probably wanted to comfort me. She always spoke her mind. It was hard not to talk after what had happened. But if she'd been fond of Vlasta — and she had been — then Fanynka would have actually resented me if she thought I were to blame for this whole calamity. So why would she want to console me? I battled with thoughts like these all night. But what worked me up the most was the memory of Kilian's bleak visions, Kilian the blind seer. His visions were more reliable than all the arguments and counter-arguments based on hard facts. Kilian sensed what was going on. He was the secret chief witness of the whole grievous affair. He was probably the only one who was able to interpret it correctly and account for my part in Vlasta's tragedy — if it was a mere part at all, that is, and I wasn't in fact the destroying angel, sent neither from Heaven nor from Hell; indeed, it is usually some poor, unfortunate heel, someone with no other purpose in life, who is condemned to play this role.

"'How's my cravat,' asked Philomena when I saw her again just a few days after these harrowing events. Because one thing is sure: I failed to catch the warnings. I didn't tell myself: This is the point where I have to turn back, to leave it all behind me. I misunderstood what Kilian was trying to tell me. I couldn't resist and went to Philomena. But, no, it isn't that simple. I couldn't resist going to Philomena the same way salmon can't resist their migration upstream. And yet it's not as simple as that either. Because I'm human, not salmon, and can't talk my way out of it by shifting the blame to the ineluctable force of nature. And yet it's not as simple as that at all. For how did I end up being human? Why do I bear this burden? Why this hardship? You have to ask, as the Disciples did: 'Who sinned, this man or his parents, that he was born blind?' And yet it is said we're all children of God."

"Careful, Weissenstein. It's not rhetorical; the prophet was posing a question. Do we not all have one Father? Were we not created by one God? So why do we despise one another and profane the Covenant that was made with our fathers?"

"Yes, indeed. Why? Well, how am *I* supposed to know? But I did have an answer ready for Philomena's question about the cravat: 'I only wear it on Sunday.' It was obviously a stupid answer, because Philomena knew for a fact that Sunday had no special meaning for me. But could I really tell *her*, this woman from whom I had always been careful to hide my relations with Vlasta, could I really tell her that her cravat was now in some drawer at police headquarters? Perhaps it would have been better to say the cravat had mysteriously disappeared, that I'd lost it or had it stolen. But justifications were never my strong point. And it's hard with invented justifications to try and insert them into reality. Even a simple and obvious justification, if it happens to be concocted, puts the whole of existence out of context. If, on the other hand, your reason happens to be true, you'll do best if it's incredibly absurd. But I only learned that up here. I wasn't aware of it at the time.

"If I had told the truth: 'A hooker, who was also my lover, hanged herself with your cravat, which is now being kept at police headquarters,' Philomena would have probably burst into laughter, would have likely given me a kiss on the cheek to thank me for the wonderful joke, and never asked about the cravat again. Instead she was deeply saddened and said: 'You don't like it?' — 'I save it for special occasions precisely because I like it,' I said, continuing my foolish justification, which was downright imbecilic if only for the simple reason that each stroll with Philomena was a special occasion and because I surely insulted her by wearing the old one again, which was slightly threadbare and unworthy of her. But had I gotten a new one there's a good chance she would have been even more offended. It was one of life's subtle and fatally hopeless conflicts. Wanting to make an elegant impression, I'd gotten myself a bamboo cane that bent just a little when I leaned on it, and donned an artistic hat that not even the most resourceful hatter could have worked back into shape. You might find it strange that I went to such lengths to look like the others and not to stand out. But every single one of these efforts had precisely the opposite effect. Herr Feldscharek used a malacca cane back then, Dr. Stein a rosewood one, and the walking stick of Rabbi Reach was ebony with a silver knob. A lot of intellectual types used walking sticks, tie-pins and signet rings. I'd even paid money for my little bamboo cane, and not without sacrifice. This was before I got the job with Masopust. I had the choice:

it was either a hash at a modest eatery or the cane that I saw in a junk shop. I deprived myself of the meal.

"But the question of the cravat soon faded into the background during a walk up at the Belvedere, when Philomena, after some hemming and hawing, began to confess she had reason to suspect she was going to become a mother.

"'How is that possible?' I screamed, and my screaming must have sounded hateful indeed. 'I haven't touched you, not since that night near Kolín.'

"'Of course you have,' she said, 'you're such a joker! I bet you could give a detailed description of every single embrace.'

"Philomena's character and way of life completely ruled out her telling a conscious lie, much less an attempt to saddle me with the consequences of a perfidious affair with someone else. And why should she? Anyone was preferable to me, no matter how you looked at it. On the other hand, I was absolutely certain that since our rustic interlude many months before I hadn't come close enough to put her in this compromising position.

"But she insisted that, time and again, I had swept her off her feet and made her blissfully happy, recounted this in a childish and soul-stirring way, got carried away depicting the sweetest of details, and proved it all with concrete allusions: 'that was back at the Vineyard Inn, you remember, you registered us as man and wife' . . . 'and then that time behind Prague Castle, in that ancient inn with the potbellied stove in the room. The maid was always disturbing us to put more wood on the fire' . . . 'and that time when . . .' and so on. I didn't dare to even mention that all of this was utterly impossible. Where would I have gotten the money to pay for romantic outings like that? And would she, Philomena, anxious and chaste as she was, would she have even been game for such ventures and their many awkward situations: the grinning doorman, the cheeky looks of chambermaids, the hotbed hotels with bug stains, musty sheets and the smell of Lysol? It never would have even occurred to me to try and talk her into such things. You ask how I'm so familiar with such places and their discomforts. Well, I've got what you might call an exact imagination. But the culmination was when Philomena said: 'And then, when you took me to your room. More of an alcove, really, but it was good enough for us, wasn't it? And now the inevitable will come, and should. I'm a little bit scared of my mother. But you'll stand by me, won't you? You won't jilt me like Faust did to Gretchen.' The fact that she compared me, Weissenstein Karl, to Faust seemed so indescribably funny to me at the time that I was seized by a fit of laughter — I say 'seized' because it soon reached an almost hysterical pitch. I had never taken Philomena to my attic room; I would have been too ashamed of its shabbiness. And still she described it in exhaustive detail: the sagging mattress, the ever-dripping faucet, the bare bulb hanging from the ceiling that you could only turn on and off by the door, and even the portrait of Aunt Karla, fastened to the wall with four pins. She took my laughter quite seriously, though, and said: 'You see, I knew you wouldn't abandon me.'

"'No, I won't,' I said, and stopped laughing, 'but I will make some inquiries. One of my acquaintances will surely know of a reliable doctor.'

"'Doctor? What do I need a doctor for? I'm perfectly fine. Everything's as it should be with me.' Suddenly she stopped and anxiously asked: 'You don't honestly think I would let anyone take it away from me, do you?'

"'Take it away? No. Heaven forbid! Of course not. But a doctor should check you anyway, to see if it's even the case.'

"'How could you doubt? I feel it and know it for sure. Everything's changing, inside and out. I've known for eight weeks.'

"'Yes, of course. I don't doubt you. Still, you need to be informed about what you should or shouldn't do.' But she laughed at me, waved it off, or said there was plenty of time still.

"I was firmly convinced that Philomena was in a state of delirium, which a medical examination would dispel, but the defining characteristic of such a state is that the sufferer has no interest in being rid of the suffering. 'I've heard of such cases of autosuggestion,' Feldscharek confirmed for me when I consulted him in my agitated state and who, staring into space over his spectacles, had me recount the whole story or, rather, Philomena's story. 'Yes, it does exist. I once knew a girl who fancied she'd grown a big belly, though in fact it was just an illusion.' He was prepared to refer me to a physician friend of his, Dr. Kantner, that's how charitable a person he was, after having seen my helplessness, indeed my near desperation. And yet he was smiling just a little. True, he always wore a faint smile, probably even when he we was sitting on the can or even when he was crying, since everyone cries sometimes, and rightly so, even Feldscharek. But this time he seemed to be smiling a little more than usual, attributing as he did the most trivial motives to me — that is to say, that I had in fact been the primitive physical cause of a simple biological process whose consequences had gone to my head and which I was now understandably trying to elude. He could understand my desperation.

"Surely I must have seemed unreliable, for Philomena's incessant talk, which became more colorful and confident each day, had thrown me off my stride so much that my certainty of not having touched her in any decisive way since that night in the countryside long ago was slowly beginning to crumble. Besides, I knew from experience that there were phases in which I felt there were two of me. Was it possible that in such a state of alterity I had made a move on Philomena and turned her into a mother? Her utterances were so precise, the facts she relished retelling so cogent and persuasive that — endeavoring to please her — I often found myself adopting her emphatic tone myself and conceding: 'Yes, that was back when we did, saw, experienced such-and-such together,' although in reality it wasn't true. Alas, my story is just as baroque, towered, domed, hilly and tinged with sadness as the city of Prague, as you can see for yourself. The terrible tragedy with Vlasta still shook me, I didn't know if I would ever get over it, didn't in fact ever want to get over it. You cannot atone for a limited time and only with part of your being; you have to atone with the whole of your existence. Sometimes I thought the new burden and sorrow that Philomena caused me was one form of my atonement.

"One morning Masopust handed me a little package

wrapped in tissue paper. It contained the claret-red tie, torn at the narrow end. 'I was with the inspector yesterday, at the Kumanovo wine bar. We always eat ćevapčići and drink Trebbiano there. He told me that the case of the beautiful tragic sinner had now been closed for good. Why, he asked, should I trouble Herr Weissenstein by making him come to headquarters? Give him his property back yourself. All he needs to do is sign the receipt.' I signed: 'Received: one torn silk cravat, property of Herr Weissenstein Karl.' I would have now turned my attention to organizing the old Engelhorn editions if Masopust, who — like many an individual — had a particular penchant for lurid details, had not started up again: 'The tie is actually as good as new; it's only torn at the narrow end which, if you knot it skillfully, won't even be visible.' That was a gruesome proposition. I must have given Masopust a creepy look, for he blanched before he turned away from me and muttered: 'Well, we had the best intentions. We wanted to spare you an unpleasant trip. The authorities, after all, can't hold on to things that don't belong to them. You can do what you want with it. You can throw the tie away for all I care.' I didn't say a thing, but went to the shelf with translations from the French and took down the second volume of a novel I almost knew by heart, which had been a kind of bible for me back when I still lived among the poets. I opened it toward the end and silently pointed to a sentence spoken by a dreaded convict who, disguised as a Spanish priest, addresses a young man who's about to take his own life: 'Never do an unsolicited favor!' Then I turned my back to Masopust and left the bookshop for good.

Perhaps I had shown a lack of humility. I know it's our human duty to accept humiliation with gratitude, always, for we always have something to atone for. But it's human destiny that atonement is never complete.

"I told Philomena about Dr. Kantner. But she kept repeating, 'There's no rush. I know how I'm doing. I'm not sick. I don't need a doctor.' I tried to explain to her the difficulties she'd encounter with those around her. 'My mother will scold me, but she'll come around eventually,' she countered. 'And my uncle? He's much too fond of me. I could even go to him when it's time.' — 'But you can't even say for sure if you're pregnant.' She merely laughed. I became enraged. 'And what about me? Just look at me! I'm no one and nothing. How am I supposed to be a father and husband? I have a right to know what's in store for me.' 'But you know that already,' she said, growing calmer the more worked up I got. Getting worked up is trivial, but calmness has something demonic about it.

"Of course no one has the right to know what's in store for him. The arrogation of such a right has engendered every misfortune and every tyranny in the world. Wanting to be like God, not accepting what comes. Don't reproach me for stating the obvious. One should never stop pointing out the many simple things that have long since been forgotten. Learning is recollection. I still hoped that Philomena was simply having hallucinations and, if not, that she would ultimately agree to an operation. I sounded out Dr. Kantner. 'Where would you get an idea like that?' he said. But I knew from Feldscharek that he was just saying that. Because after regarding me at length — I'm tempted to say: after studying me — Dr. Kantner said: 'The important thing is that the young lady comes to me sooner than later.' He knew my situation was desperate, that I was little more than a supplicant. Today I realize that's no reason to feel depressed. Anyone who thinks they're not a supplicant is simply being presumptuous. We do not live by justice, but by grace. I didn't come up with this principle, and it's often been said before by those who have managed to penetrate to the heart of the matter. I prayed that Philomena would decide to go see Dr. Kantner. But therein lay my blindness. For it's wrong to complain about something like that. We know, after all, what we're allowed to ask for at best: life, purity, and atonement for the wrongs we've committed. It's preposterous to want to give God suggestions: Do this or that! If anything we should pray like this: Hallowed be thy name! Thy will be done! Thy kingdom come!

"Sometimes I thought I should maybe turn to you for help. You were newly married and might have known what to do. I was afraid, however, of any kind of advice. Because following someone's advice was just a way of shifting the blame. I incapacitate myself, put myself under tutelage, do what the other deems important — and ultimately saddle him with my burden, the one I was meant to carry. No one should be allowed to act if they can't make up their own minds. Though that's easier said than done, for the essential and decisive things in life do not proceed from us, but from somewhere else entirely. They say that most men are glad to become a father. Hopefully it really is that way, I'd like to believe it is. It's the moment they sense their likeness to God. They run the risk of Creation, God's risk, all over again. It can all go very wrong. But God at least had the Babel of tongues, the Flood, and His redeeming Steward. What does humankind have? What do I have? Shouldn't I be mortified of fatherhood? Do you remember how our generation read Kierkegaard? Granted, I never understood him. I wasn't worthy. But the titles alone were tremendously exciting and convincing enough for me. *Fear and Trembling, The Sickness Unto Death, Either/Or*. Humanness, provided it's not merely animal, springs from paradox. Our most fervent desire is what we fear the most, and vice versa. It's none too surprising that a person suddenly dies the moment his dream comes true. He dies of fear, just as happiness might do him in when something long feared actually comes to pass. When it comes to human affairs, who would dare sit in judgment?

"To put it in more ordinary terms, my misfortune was that one day I encountered Dr. Kantner on Kastulusgasse. Of course I'm being impudent again by calling it a misfortune, and anyway I'm not being honest, for I didn't encounter him by chance, but was drawn to the street in the very hope of catching him there after hours. If you wanted to be wholly sincere, you'd have to recant or at least correct every sentence you've ever uttered or wrote, for language is a constant source of corruption and confusion. Make of that what you will. 'Now then,' said Dr. Kantner to me, 'how's your little bride? I'm expecting her next Wednesday at two in the afternoon.' He uttered this like a command, as if he had said to me: 'Go and wash in the pool of Siloam!' And this is how in the evening I passed it on to

Philomena. The tone wasn't mine, and not even Dr. Kantner's. It came from somewhere else, which is why Philomena did not resist, and I didn't have to press her or plead with her very much at all. She said: 'Yes, I'll go. I've wanted to go all along! I'm ready now.' She said it with infinite sadness.

"'You act like you're being led to the slaughter. I just want what's best!' I shouldn't have said that. For as soon as I said the word 'slaughter' I thought of the cattle requisitioned during the war, their bellowing as they approached the slaughterhouse and began to smell its air of death, the gigantic look in their eyes on the platform of the livestock scale, the final station before their end. And then, what exactly was I trying to say: 'I just want what's best!' Best for whom? A person like me shouldn't want anything at all. Because everything he touches ends up going south.

"I later asked myself why it had to be that Wednesday that Dr. Kantner set the appointment, and why at two in the afternoon. I understood why Philomena no longer put up a fight. Something inside her was decided, or settled, she had moved beyond the trivial measures and arrangements of life, could carry them out or endure them without affecting the essence of things. And so she submitted unflinchingly to that fateful day when at precisely one-thirty in the afternoon a car drove along the riverfront under the Belvedere, Philomena having just descended the hill on her way to Dr. Kantner. Behind the wheel of the automobile sat a man in his middle years, an utterly harmless and good-natured fellow who in no way transgressed the law, neither in letter nor in spirit, who had no business to attend to at that hour and was therefore in no particular rush, but rather — as he himself declared when questioned — was simply driving for pleasure. 'But you must have had some destination in mind,' inquired the official conducting the interrogation. 'Yes, it's likely,' said the man, horrified that all of this had had to happen to him of all people, 'but I couldn't say where anymore.' — 'And why were you driving at that particular time of day?' — 'It could have just as well been an hour earlier or later, I suppose. Or even just five minutes or five seconds earlier or later. Then this whole disaster would have never happened. And, anyway, the poor girl could have crossed the street half a minute earlier or later for that matter.'

"But the course of events wouldn't have it any other way and insisted on this half a minute, these very thirty seconds. Philomena, emerging from the Belvedere park, must have been in a tremendous hurry when she suddenly stepped into the riverside road. Evidently she'd been at home, putting off the trip to Dr. Kantner from one minute to the next, that's the way I see it. She probably made this or that superfluous gesture, one too few or one too many, should not have smoothed the bedcovers or closed the wardrobe door, or should have lingered in front of the mirror just a few minutes longer, for life depends on such brief moments. Or maybe she calculated each of her movements and every chore precisely, who knows? All we know is she was in a hurry, even though she still had plenty of time to get to Dr. Kantner on time. So she must have been rushing for some other reason, toward some other objective. Eyewitnesses proved the driver's absolute innocence. He had neither been driving too fast nor had he failed to honk the horn, he obeyed the traffic rules and was driving in the right direction — meaning it really was the case that Philomena, quite inexplicably, ran, leapt or slipped directly under the wheels of the car as if she'd been drawn by a magnet. That's how the various witnesses put it. Surely the driver had done his best to swerve or brake at the very last moment. But Philomena followed the swerving vehicle as if she'd been hypnotized.

"'Like a sleepwalker,' people said.

"'As if on purpose.'

"'As if she'd been set on doing it.'

"I could have attested that she hadn't been set on doing it. She was much too kind to implicate an innocent stranger in disaster. But maybe that's just a primitive notion and no one is enough of a stranger, no one is innocent enough not to have their fair share of the world's misfortune. Grotesquely enough, I learned all of this the next morning while reading the *Prager Tagblatt*, after a night full of dreadful doubts. For Philomena had not kept our evening appointment, at which she was supposed to tell me how everything had turned out. I figured she hadn't gone to Dr. Kantner after all and didn't dare to show her face. Indeed, even a nothing like me can be so conceited at times to think that a creature like Philomena 'didn't dare' to look him in the eye. Another possibility was that Dr. Kantner had told her she wasn't pregnant at all and now she either felt ashamed and considered herself a fool or had fallen into infinite sadness and desperation; or maybe she was afraid I would think she'd feigned her condition in order to crown herself with a halo. The third possibility was that Dr. Kantner had confirmed her pregnancy and she didn't show up for our date because she'd vowed to become a mother at any cost and no matter what, or maybe because she had suddenly grasped the full import of the situation and had decided not to become a mother, which filled her in turn with a feeling of disgrace and rancor toward me. I contemplated all of this in a hundred variations that night. Only one thing didn't occur to me, something I would learn about the very next morning from a notice in the paper, and even this by chance, for I didn't even have the money to buy myself a newspaper. Each morning I went to the lobby of the newspaper building, where the morning edition was hung on the walls, and I combed the ads for work. There I read a piece of news under the heading 'local,' which normally didn't interest me but that morning caught my eye, just to show me that the important things, light or dark, are never quite where we expect them.

"I rushed to her mother, who wasn't exactly happy to see me. Truth be told, I can't say she even recognized me. She was rigid and waxen, her clothes seemingly sewn in place, her hands lying wooden on the armrests of her chair, whose expressionless carvings she seemed to be a part of, her lips disappearing inward. I stood there saying nothing. I probably seemed as stiff as she did. Some time elapsed. She sat, I stood. Even though she said nothing, I sensed she made no causal connection between me and the death of her daughter. I wished she would have, and had cursed me for it. I wish I had possessed the strength to confess: 'Pressured by me, your daughter set out to a certain place on a certain day at a certain hour which led to her demise. I'm guilty, for I led her astray. Regardless of how it happened, I was the one who planted the poison. I'm guilty simply because I exist.' But I didn't say it, probably because it would have been an arrogant exaggeration, a sign of taking myself too seriously. And she could have answered: 'I am too. Who are you to want to steal my pound of guilt? I'm not alone in this either. Don't you know how many things in the universe have to come together, in the past and now and even in the future, just for a glass to break? How many more when it comes to a human being?' And so we both remained silent.

"As I joined the cemetery procession, walking behind Philomena's bier at a certain distance from her mother and relatives, including her uncle from Kolín, my old doubts had long been replaced by new ones. I was plagued by the question of whether Philomena really had been pregnant, if the life of a second creature had ended along with hers, a creature for whose emergence and hence disappearance I myself was to blame, or if Philomena's death had been hers alone. She had been convinced she was a mother, but now I would never know if in fact she really had been. A stranger like me would never have access to the results of the forensic investigation, and so I would never find out just where I stood in life. Had I been a father or not? I would also never know — no one could know for sure — if Philomena's accident had not been a suicide after all, perhaps not minutely planned and pondered but the result of a split-second decision that arose, ripened and was carried out just as the automobile of factory owner Mitgang appeared like a phantom in front of her. That I was under no suspicion, indeed that no one bore me even the slightest grudge, became clear to me at the cemetery gates when Philomena's uncle turned up unexpectedly beside me. Not that he said anything. He merely looked at me and tapped his finger on my claret-red cravat as if to ask: 'Who wears a thing like that to a funeral?' He couldn't have known I was wearing it just for Philomena, for the second and last time.

"So basically everyone dear to me had been swept away by death and disappeared from my life. I alone was still alive. It almost seemed as if my life did not consist in my being there, but in all of those who were closest to me no longer being there, that I myself was a blank spot in the picture of existence. I was destitute back then. But it made my life easier. Perhaps that sounds like blasphemy, and doesn't conform to the moldy doctrine of socialists. Still, it was true in my case. Being destitute is below the threshold of poverty. Poverty means having just enough to stave off dire hunger. Destitution means not even having that. I know you're one of those people who at least have a rough idea of what that means. You once told me that when you were a child your supper was often little more than a slice of dark rye and ten prunes, save for a couple of smacks on the head every now and then. To me that's still luxury, a privilege of the higher classes. Destitution is more severe. Still, it's not all sorrow and lament. It can also be a form of atonement and compensation. It tears us away from the artificial, the distorted and the superfluous. It's not true that someone who is destitute hates life. The path to life's sources and its meaning is more open than at the buffets of affluence, which block the way like a barricade. Still, we strive to escape a state of destitution. Not just because we're hungry — that's true only for the more primitive cases of unmindful destitution, which, unfortunately, are rather numerous — but because dwelling unprotected in the fiercely unclouded clarity of existence is unbearable.

"I mentioned already that I followed the help-wanted ads in the lobby of the newspaper building. But ever since I ran across the news of Philomena's death, I didn't go back there anymore. I came to realize that my going there was not about finding a job, but only to see that dreadful notice printed in the local news section. My morning trips to the newspaper office fulfilled their purpose. Besides, the thought of working for the rapidly accruing wealth of some Herr XYZ filled me with a sense of loathing, a loathing more intense than my state of destitution.

"In a situation and state of mind like that, someone like me does not seek admittance to the world of the wealthy to beg for work or even for help; he consorts with the poorest of the poor instead. It was blind Kilian who knew what to do. 'If you can't work for the living, work for the dead. I know of a job for you, and you need a job to eat and forget. A person has to eat, otherwise what's the point of hunger. And a person has to forget, too, in order for him to remember.' — 'What kind of a job do you have in mind?' — 'Go to the gravediggers at Malvazinky, they'll take you.' — 'That's hard work. And I'm not in very good shape. How do you know they'll even take me?' — 'It's not so hard. You have some experience too. You worked for a funeral home once, didn't you.' — 'That was decoration. Digging real graves is a different matter.' — 'You'll get used to it, and it's healthy, too. Out all day in the fresh air. A real sanatorium, and not badly paid either. Go there tomorrow and ask for Franta Panenka, he's the one in charge there. Just yesterday I told him about you.'

"Panenka was rosy as a Christmas-tree apple and cheerful in a way that might seem out of place to someone unfamiliar with his line of work. He looked at me and shook his head. 'Only a blind man would recommend something like that,' he said, which didn't sound too encouraging. 'We'll just have to be careful,' he laughed, 'and make sure you don't bury yourself by accident.' This basically meant I'd been hired. 'You'll be the twelfth man. I could get the job done with eleven, but twelve is a good number. The twelve apostles, twelve months in a year, twelve days between Christmas and Epiphany. You look like a Jew to me, but who's asking.' I was just about to say something when he asked: 'Here's some money, go get yourself a decent meal for starters and come back tomorrow morning.' Panenka was what the Czechs call a *fotr*, a word derived from the German *Vater* (father) and means good-natured to the core, but sharp as a tack, shrewd and witty. I went and ate and overate, so much so that come next morning I felt much worse than the day before, and yet I would have rather died than not report to Panenka on time. 'Eat your fill for another day, you poor bastard,' he said 'I can't even look at you.' I thought I would have to kiss him for that and probably made to do so, because he said, 'Come now,' and had something in his eyes that reminded me of the Scriptures where it says: Whatever you have done for the least of your brothers, you have done for me. The least of the twelve, that was surely me now.

"On the third day I was part of the gang, started digging and carrying the boards they place across the grave, readying the ropes and pulleys they use to lower the coffin, and fetching the two or three trowels the mourners use to toss their clod of earth onto the dead. I saw a lot of earth, but no one ever told me what it actually is — I don't mean its composition, the scientific part, I mean how a piece always stays in your hands, dust from the star we walk on. When the whole graveside miserere was over I would help refill the hole and build a mound on top of it, after I'd picked out the stones and pebbles, for the earth shouldn't weigh on a dead person any heavier than it is already. Then the whole thing was more or less flattened, and square-cut pieces of turf were sometimes arranged on top and everything cleaned up around it, depending on how much was paid, since there are different degrees of being dead. But even if the fee was lower, we still made a point of doing our job, there was just a little less fanfare, but no one got short shrift with Panenka.

"It was quite an interesting and varied profession. We grave-diggers had the dead with us, we had the survivors, and we often had the long-forgotten dead too, whose graves we opened if the fee wasn't paid and when space was needed for new arrivals. There we found the remains of old coffins and the withered, crumbling bones, the skulls and jaws of the dead, which we wrapped up in an old cloth and reinterred at the foot of the grave. It reminded me of Hamlet sometimes, and the time I heard Herr Moissi conversing with the gravediggers once, back when I used to run with the poets. Panenka, or whichever one of us happened to be there, would occasionally snap up an old wedding ring or pendant earring — nothing too valuable, so don't go thinking there was any harm in it. They had a tacit agreement not to talk about these things, not even to notice it, for sooner or later it was everyone's turn, and ultimately it was only fair if the uselessly wealthy dead gave some of their abundance to the living poor. Only the living can meaningfully possess things. You don't wander around through eternal bliss wearing rings or brooches. Panenka and his men were no hyenas; they were archaeologists of sorts. We ran across other oddities, too. I once unearthed a half-rotted wig. The wig had belonged to a man. Who was he trying to fool down there in the dark, dank earth?

"I soon felt so at home in this new world of mine that Panenka asked the cemetery administration to let me sleep in the wooden shed where we kept the wheelbarrows and tools that were used in our macabre line of work. All the other employees were married, and somebody had to watch over the tools and keep them in working order. I moved in with my battered vulcanized-fiber suitcase that Herr Werfel had given me once in Leipzig. It contained, apart from my underwear, a copy of Werfel's *The Friend of the World*, Bezruč's *Silesian Songs*, *The Metamorphosis*, and Březina's *Mysterious Distances*. I pinned to the wooden wall the pastel portrait of my aunt, thus transforming my little corner into a veritable castle. Panenka had been kind enough to provide me with an iron cot. 'Procházka slept that way all his life,' he said, 'and he almost made it to the age of ninety.' Procházka is how the Czechs referred to Emperor Franz Joseph.

"After work I studied the gravestones, these curious formations of sandstone or granite, limestone or marble, bronze or cast iron, with crosses, urns or angel statues, and sometimes with porcelain ovals depicting in fading but still recognizable photographic reproductions the faces of those buried there. They 'rested in peace' or 'with God,' were 'beloved,' 'gone but not forgotten,' the 'eternal light' illuminated their titles, honors, merits and often multiple positions within the family, all carefully chiseled in stone or cast in bronze. Some graves had nothing written on them. All they had was a number. Their names had vanished, their deeds were unknown, and hopefully their misdeeds forgiven. Whether we've lived like this or like that: everyone dies, and rightly so. No sooner have the priests, the servers and family members departed, have the horns faded away and the wreaths begun to unravel than the business of transformation sets in, profoundly and gradually, for everyone. The pomp of names, gravestones and titles is meant to link the dead with life and the living as long as possible, which is why the graves are kept looking presentable, the damaged ones repaired, crooked ones straightened, the rust and mildew carefully scrubbed from all these memorial stones. But I don't think you're really assisting the dead in the execution of their new and utterly different duties. I would often spend an entire hour, sitting at an unmarked grave and listening without even thinking, bestowing on it my mere existence, not touching the grass or the flowers or laying hands on what people call weeds, as if they knew one from the other. It seems to me that these hours were the only time in my life I didn't sin. For the sake of these hours, have mercy on me, holy justice! When everyone had left, at six o'clock, the cemetery became a mere landscape. It had tall trees aplenty with birds and small animals, and some spots had a view of nearby hills overlooking the city. I was safe here from the eagerness of others. Either you hurt them or they hurt you. It's rare that no one gets hurt, and only in the case of complete indifference. I got along well with my fellow gravediggers during working hours. They were quite a different sort than, say, construction workers or coal miners. A construction worker can always be struck dead by a beam, a miner killed by explosions, cave-ins or floods. Death can be lurking right around the corner. They know that but don't always think about it. But these gravediggers had no disasters to fear. And yet every day and every hour the thought of death was ever present. Death was unceasing for them, it never died, so to speak. Not a day went by when graves were not in need of digging. And though these gravediggers may have spent their lunch break sitting on planks by a hole in the ground, consuming sausage and pastries just like other workmen did, still there was something philosophical about them, and necessarily so, on account of their constant proximity to death.

"I underwent three phases with them. First they were skittish and unapproachable, and hardly said a word to me, conversing among themselves in their cemetery jargon, a language they themselves had invented or perhaps had inherited from previous generations of gravediggers. A grave was called a 'hole,' a dead person was a 'has-been,' burying was referred to as 'wrapping up,' and when they had to make a mound they'd say: 'Let the bun rise, we can still hear him coughing.' Later they began to pull my leg, to tease and kid me whenever they could. That was a little better. Finally they came to accept me, since they realized I was useful, in different ways to each of them. I knew they'd included me in their little circle when they started calling me 'Pumpkinhead.' It wasn't meant as an insult at all. After all, my enormous head was truly my defining characteristic. And, anyway, they all called each other by bodily or animal nicknames: Kulhánek the 'limper,' Nosatý the 'nosy,' one was called Bottleneck, another Walleye, and yet another Pig Ear. Only Panenka forever remained Panenka. But one day they called me Pumpkinhead, which is when I knew I was part of the gang. In the beginning I made an ass of myself, since I thought those nicknames were actually their real names and always referred to them as 'Mr. Bottleneck' or 'Mr. Pig Ear.' That almost got me punched in the nose, since they thought I was making fun of them. But soon they noticed how seriously I took them. At that point they became friendly.

"'You should spend more time around people,' said Bottleneck one day, 'I don't mean dead ones, I mean the living.'

"'Yeah, you spend all your time digging graves or in the shed,' Limper concurred. 'You may as well be dead.'

"'You need other people to live,' added Walleye, 'you need to take care, 'cause the day you're only concerned with yourself will be the day you die.'

"'Then there'd be nothing but corpses running around,' said Pig Ear, and Nosy added that this was already the case. But Panenka interrupted this conversation, saying: 'Keep your wisdom to yourself. Pumpkinhead's finally putting on weight, the work here seems to agree with him. He's got some color now. What more do you want?'

"He was right. But appearances can be deceiving. I was merely bracing myself for death. I always knew that blind Kilian could see what was coming. My cemetery days were merely a phase of preparation, they were only temporary. I searched my soul and recognized that the reason I always transformed myself was because I was born without the courage to actually be myself. My appearance, my face, the tone of my voice had always belied whatever I said or did. No one ever believed Weissenstein Karl, no matter how earnest or true. And so, not yet ripe for true humility, I underwent transformations. The crucial precondition for humility is courage.

"I often stood at Vlasta's graveside when no one else was left at the cemetery. I stood there in my wrongness and waited. What are you waiting for? For someone to come and lighten your load? Are you still looking for justifications? Are you still scraping together the few tiny things in your life in the hope of them working to your advantage on the scales of the angels of judgment? Wasn't it true that even the good you thought you had done was basically stolen and didn't come from within, but was merely borrowed and imitated? When did you ever do more than simply save yourself and put on airs in front of others and even in front of yourself? Even your search is immodest and sinful, your renunciation presumptuousness, your self-castigation tantamount to robbing God. Don't you see that you have no choice but to surrender yourself to the angel of judgment and beg for mercy from him? You can go on living and keep on defending yourself, but this defense, no matter how sound your arguments, is still as hopeless as the life that feeds off it. Stop sinning with your defense and be prepared!

"Mark my words, there is indeed an angel of judgment just like there's a guardian angel. Most importantly, though, it's not two separate angels — for numbers cease to exist in those spheres — but one and the same. First I guard you, then I judge you. The guardian angel becomes the angel of judgment. No one dies as a mere piece of flesh, as a heap of exhausted cells. Not even scientists or insurance agents, or communists for that matter, believe that in their heart of hearts. And I beg you: When you write down my words, just don't make them Expressionist, nothing poetistic, and no magic realism either, or whatever they call those cowardly attempts to flee from truth into form. Don't make style out of sentence fragments, out of missing predicates and free rhythms. Write it all down in ordinary prose and, I beg you, scream into people's ears: 'There is a God, because there's an angel of judgment and I, Weissenstein Karl, have seen him!' If you're unable to shout then whisper, and if you can't whisper then try to convince them some other way. There are so many ways. You'll find a way somehow!

"Everyone had gone home already. I was alone between the graves. That's when he came — not with radiant wings, not with scales, not with a flowing gown, and not with a shining countenance. A simple being, with no distinguishing characteristics, because he blends into every environment at any given moment. People would have taken him for a belated cemetery visitor, a not particularly grief-stricken mourner who stuck around after the last burial service. Of course he didn't start questioning me, sounding me out and probing my conscience. And yet still there's something eerie about him, speaking as he does about other things entirely, and seemingly in passing: about the weather, the position of the sun, the peculiar smell that only plants on graves exude. I began to pray: 'Mother comes home from the fields. Her eyes are weak and wearied from work. She wants to thread a needle but, try as she might, the poor thing can't get the thread through the needle.'

"'That's a good prayer,' said the angel of judgment. 'Take a good look at the sun. Evening's upon us. And tomorrow it's going to rain. It won't be bothering you. You'll proceed toward the spring of your youth. But the fact that rain is coming gives it all a special feeling. Savor it. The thyme and mint are hard at work. Nature, my friend, is full of pleasant details. She differentiates so beneficently between what is important and what is not. Don't be concerned about resurrection. It's the easiest thing in the world, a shrewd wise man once discerned, because being born a second time is no more surprising than the first. I take it you have no complaints? That's how it should be. For those who complain only keep their dissatisfaction alive longer than they need to.'

"'Well,' I thought to myself, 'that would be my death notice.

And luckily my passing will be of no concern to others, or only just a little. I won't be leaving behind any grief.'

"'That means truly dying,' said the being, vanishing into the bushes. I'm amazed how smoothly everything went. No sickness or struggle. I always knew it would be wholly different from the way I ever imagined it. Death is the unimaginable, and life is the inability to ever imagine death. No language is up to the task. It's like with God Himself. Don't even go to the trouble, please.

"From this point on I can only speak as an outside observer, to the edifice of the world or — forgive me — from and to. I had fallen onto Vlasta's grave and lay there until the dewy morning when Limper and Bottleneck showed up. The two men lived in Košíře, in the very same building, and stuck together like two old cronies. They found me lying there and immediately began their ridiculous attempts at resuscitation, which, had I still been alive, would have surely been highly unpleasant. But, as things stood, my senses were gone and the two of them could devote themselves to a full half hour of their first-aid efforts without in the least disturbing me. Realizing it was pointless, they eventually summoned the others, who had meanwhile turned up for work and now paired up to try yet again to revive my earthly remains by performing their gymnastics on me. Rarely in my lifetime had I gotten so much exercise, except perhaps with Paul Adler, blessed be his memory, when we ran through the night around Hellerau, leaping over hedges, ditches and furrows. 'Faster, Weissenstein, faster!' Panenka arrived in the meantime and discovered the fine little mess they were in. 'We have to call the doctor,' he said, 'because no one just drops dead like that. He has to determine a cause of death.'

"It was, as predicted, a damp, rainy morning. My coworkers were huddled like a choir around my corpse. But that was soon more than they could bear. They carried me into the shed and laid me on the mattress beneath the portrait of Aunt Karla. Though graves and corpses and dug-up remains were actually their daily bread and death an everyday occurrence to them, they were nonetheless deeply affected by my passing, for death, in me, had come right between them — I was one of them, after all — and I noticed with some satisfaction that now, as a consequence, I'd become each one of them. They stood around and leaned around in silence for a while until their own uneasiness began to make them feel self-conscious, and so they attempted the occasional joke, harmlessly poking fun at my way of being or speaking, just as they'd done with the living me. It was as if they wanted to keep me alive, at least for a little while longer. Eventually the medical official from Smíchov arrived, saw right away that I was dead, felt my pulse all the same, listened with his stethoscope, an object he seemed to be proud of, and immediately grew flustered — I couldn't help noticing — when the moment he bent down over my corpse a button popped off his underwear, which now slipped down to unfathomable depths. As a doctor he also did one more thing: plucked a blade of grass from outside the door of the shed and ran it over my pupils. At this point I might well have scared him by twitching, not because I was still alive but because, for some inexplicable reason, my rigor mortis had not yet set in and killed every reflex in my body. But I abstained from playing this prank on him, considering that he was an elderly man with an even more elderly wife who'd henpecked his very existence. Finally he straightened himself, reaching first into his pants and pulling up the offending garment, not without considerable effort and dancer-like movements. Then he proclaimed resoundingly: 'Dead!' Everyone nodded approvingly, the whole procedure having taken much too long. 'Dead is dead,' announced Panenka, as if the doctor's diagnosis wasn't valid without his personal seal of approval.

"'What's his name,' asked the doctor, 'where does he live, what's his religion, who are his next of kin, where are his papers?' Panenka gave him my legal name. Pumpkinhead would have been fine by me. He drew a blank, though, with the remaining questions. Papers? There were none. So the doctor issued a provisional death certificate for one 'Weissenstein Karl.' The authorities would see to the rest.

"'What should we do with him now?' asked Panenka.

"'Well, you can bury him somewhere temporarily once the waiting period is over and until they determine where he belongs.'

"So when the time had come, they dug me a grave along the wall. Then they placed me in a roughly-hewn box, which was anyway the perfect receptacle for me. Before they nailed the lid on, though, Bottleneck made one last suggestion:

"'We should dress him in the red tie. It would look more respectable.' And so he began to do it himself, instructing himself as he did so in order to buck himself up: 'First lay the two ends side by side, then wrap the right one around the other, thread it through the top from behind like that, and draw up the knot with the other end . . .'

"'Watch out you don't strangle him,' cautioned Limper. They laughed a little but not too much. 'I just want to hide the torn end,' explained Bottleneck. When the working day had come to an end, they lowered me into the grave.

"'Well, now we've finally wrapped him up,' said Panenka, 'gladly, too, and with all of our heart. Here he lies temporarily, but on Judgment Day they'll know where he belongs and what the point of it was.'

"Then each of them tossed onto my casket the customary trowelful of dirt, before laying into it with the bigger shovels, piling up the mound and pressing the top and sides smooth with boards, even hauling in some gray-green turf which they placed on top of the soil.

"'He gets it for free' — those were Panenka's last words about me, and they sounded like a prayer.

"And so I lay and still lie, the police having soon given up their search to establish my identity. 'He's buried and that's that,' said the inspector from Smíchov. 'What business is it of ours if maybe he was a Jew, let alone a Protestant.' They kept my file in an office in Smíchov. That much is definite. And so I've been resting in peace, temporarily, with nothing but Catholics for thirty-five years now. The grass has since grown over me, untold rain showers have swept across us, and we've rotted together in harmony.

"So this would be the story Herr Werfel asked you to write. It's all still very provisional, and has been since my birth, or probably even well before it. I may be wrong, but to me it kind of seems that everyone's story, the history of the entire world in fact, is nothing but one big makeshift arrangement otherwise known as LIFE."

RIGHT PANEL

The Legacy of a Young Man

One day — the First World War was blazing on every front, but the war had nothing directly to do with the human events I'm about to relate — one day the writers at Café Arco were buzzing with excitement. There was talk that Heinrich Mann was intending to visit Prague and give a lecture. He had chosen to speak on Émile Zola, less as a literary phenomenon than as a crusader against the moral crisis afflicting the community of nations and states. They debated amongst themselves how to give Heinrich Mann a worthy reception. "Why don't you all go to the station and give him a good welcome? I could give him roses," suggested lovely Wanda. She was the daughter of a typesetter who worked at a local Prague paper. Although she had only attended grade school, she had learned entire pages of Kierkegaard by heart in order to impress her lover, the sharp-witted literary critic P.; without understanding a word of what she was saying, she would recite these passages out of the blue at the café table. "Man is spirit. But what is spirit? Spirit is the self. But what is the self? The self is a relation which relates itself to its own self; the self is not the relation but consists of the fact that the relation relates itself to its own self. Man is a synthesis of the infinite and the finite, of the temporal and the eternal, of freedom and necessity, in short it is a synthesis. A synthesis is a relation between two factors. So regarded, man is not yet a self." And then she would add: "That's the way it is, end of story!"

"Okay, okay, we know you're an expert when it comes to relations," sneered Walter Fürth with his mop of curly hair and whose claim to fame was having started working on a novella which to date only consisted of one line: "Walter F. had inherited nothing from his father except the curse of living." — "But," frizzy-haired Fürth went on, "the important thing right now is doing something for Heinrich Mann. Oh, how I suffer!" Almost everything he said ended with a pained expression on his face and his signature remark: "Oh, how I suffer!"

"A splendid young lady," said the full-bearded Czech Antonín Macek, a mild-mannered Social Democratic author who was so hard of hearing that he could never follow a conversation. His gaze rested adoringly on Wanda's figure. "A splendid young lady, and what magnificent views she has!"

"Heinrich Mann," muttered Weissenstein, the world reformer, "the liberation of the oppressed is inevitable!" Weissenstein saw this liberation advancing on every front.

Kafka, infinitely remote, smiled and said nothing. "When is he supposed to come," asked the benevolent, blind Oskar Baum. "Werfel or Max Brod could give speeches."

"Excellent," said Fürth, "Max Brod can speak for the older generation. After all, he's in his early thirties now. Does no one know how I suffer?"

No one bothered to answer. Werfel was only listening with one ear. When suddenly a tall female figure with snow-white hair but an extremely youthful and strikingly beautiful countenance became visible outside on the street, he rose as if in a trance, abandoned his coffee and half-eaten walnut crescent pastry and vanished without having paid. Headwaiter Poschta was used to this and blithely put it on his tab.

"As your sweet ways enraptured me to death and I through you in space soared far away," Weissenstein began to recite.

"Yeah, yeah, jesting yet again about the infinite," observed Kisch. The "raging reporter," as people called him, had returned to his hometown on a brief furlough from the front.

"Yesterday Alice G. was here," said Weissenstein, beginning to interpret his own recitation, "and she said that the woman, the white-haired goddess, walked on water, as it were, with her eyes closed. That there's always an angel beside her. It's the vision of the way she walks that turns him into a poet."

"Oh, please," interjected a peevish Wanda. "You men should see what women do when they're alone. But what about this Heinrich Mann?"

"We should get down on our knees and worship him," said an ardent Karl Brand to himself, but his words were still referring to Werfel. Young Brand was always ardent, emotionally and physically. Consumption was galloping away with him, and he was always in a fever. He had chosen his nom de plume carefully, Brand meaning "fire" or "blaze." He was ceaselessly burning.

"Among the prose artists of our day," began the sharp-witted critic P., who also happened to be a bank clerk, "Heinrich Mann is the one who, with the élan of a great raconteur, has carried over into the German literary sphere the art of brilliant psychological characterization, which is otherwise the preserve of the French. It is he who has kept Expressionism from drifting into the insubstantial. He's the quintessential combination of the aesthetic and the ethical."

"Besides which he married the daughter of a Bohemian factory owner, I believe," Kafka added softly.

"What magnificent views," said old Macek, who of course hadn't understood a word. Fürth sighed: "Oh, how I suffer!" Whereas Wanda, for her part, sniffed yet another opportunity.

"The ethical as such," she declared "is the universal. It reposes immanently in itself, it has nothing without itself which is its *telos*, but is itself *telos* for everything outside it. Period."

No one seemed to heed Wanda's remarks, and so she grumbled angrily: "What's the matter? Why don't you say something? It's a quote from *Fear and Trembling*. Say something at least. Even if it's just: Go to hell!"

"We're not about to introduce the Spanish court ceremonial for your sake," said Kisch.

Kafka, who never stayed long at the café, stood up and took his leave, bowing politely to each and every one of us, then walked away with his long, increasingly lonely stride.

Brand, too, got ready to leave. I accompanied him. Over his gaunt figure he wore an Inverness cape, a garment that was utterly anachronistic even then but which he'd received as a hand-me-down from his father. Brand was poor. His father worked in a bakery. His mother was a domestic servant. His sister was employed in an office. He had graduated from a commercial college and had hoped, before the war broke out, to land a job in Egypt. He had always dreamed of the South. It could have meant his convalescence. But the war had foiled those plans. Meanwhile Brand's condition had deteriorated to such an extent that practicing a profession was out of the question. The need to take what had been denied to him, the unattainable, and mold it into something real from the material of the mind had made him a poet almost by necessity. Dreams became the very substance of his life, and the images of these dreams — renunciation, desire, rebellion against his physical decline — became the leitmotif of his message to the world. He was looking for a role model, striving for comparisons. And so he entered our circle. Werfel, or someone, usually paid his meager tab, as was the case with the even more destitute Weissenstein. Werfel likely helped Brand out in other ways too from time to time, and so Brand looked up to him as if he were a messenger of the gods. Hadn't Werfel hinted recently that he would recommend Brand's work to the great publisher of the Expressionists in Leipzig? Was he not planning some kind of fundraiser to help get Brand into a sanatorium in South Tyrol or maybe even in Switzerland? With a burning, languishing look in his eyes, Brand gazed at the girls in the full bloom of youth who sometimes sat at our table: at Wanda (cynically referred to by Fürth as the "tribune of the plebs"), at Milena, the emotional and clever-hearted young woman, at the moonlike magic of the actress Martha N., and at others who occasionally turned up and disappeared again, Elysian visitors who bestowed on

Brand's friends affection and probably loving embraces, but at best had only gentle compassion or kindness left over for Brand.

"Why does everyone always laugh at Wanda when she quotes Kierkegaard," said Brand, as we walked through Old Town toward Charles Bridge. "I think what she does is admirable. What passion it must take to mindlessly memorize entire pages just because she hopes to please Herr P. with it. I can only imagine what it feels like to be loved by a woman so intensely! And utterly in vain, only by virtue of the absurd. Because for ages now he's only had eyes for Milena, like most of the others."

"That's the difference, I guess, between those who are naturally irresistible," I answered, "and those who hope to achieve their aim by way of sacrifice. Wanda would have a much greater allure if she would simply sit there and do nothing."

"She's magnificent the way she is, even if she hasn't got the slightest idea what the word *telos* means. What does it mean, anyway?"

"It means 'aim,' 'purpose.'"

"Aha. Aim. Purpose. Do you think Wanda would read books with me if someone asked her to? It was just an idea I had. I mean so I could explain some things to her so she at least knows what she's talking about. I don't know much myself, of course. The word *telos*, for example, I didn't know that one. But maybe I could give her a little assistance, help her in her amorous endeavors."

"Why don't you suggest it to her."

"Me? No, I could never do that. Someone else would have to do it for me."

"I'll do it," I promised.

"Thank you. But won't I be repugnant to her? I'm sick, after all. I cough. Sometimes blood comes up. It might be contagious. She would find it repellent. And rightly so."

"Nonsense. First, you'll soon get better. Second, she sits with you often enough at the same table at Arco anyway. Third, she likes you."

"Really? You think so? Oh, you're just saying that. And as for getting better, good heavens, how could I ever get better? I know exactly how long it will take till I cough up the rest of my lung. I can count the months on my fingers. You know, when I lie there at night and look out the window at the moon, or simply into the black void, I start to count, and I count from one coughing spell to the next. My veins swell and my breathing sounds like a chorus of croaking frogs. Then I might turn on the light and keep track of my counting by writing it down, or I fantasize about a woman who'd once been mine before I lost her, we would even have a child together, a woman who loved me to the point of hatred and that I hated back with equal fervor."

As he spoke we crossed the midway point of the venerable Charles Bridge with its avenue of Baroque saint statues. On the sidewalk opposite two gentlemen were coming toward us, the poets Friedrich Adler and Hugo Salus. Both of them belonged to the erstwhile "liberal era" of Prague German literature. Brand and I doffed our hats with a respectful bow, despite the fact that, in our opinion, the two doctors were has-beens when it came to poetry. Salus, with his long wavy poet's locks flowing down to the nape of his neck and his black poet's necktie fluttering from his stand-up collar, nodded to us condescendingly.

"Salus rei publicae suprema lex esto," I said to Brand, who admittedly didn't understand any Latin. "That's a quote from Cicero, and you know how I would translate it? Let the supreme laws of the state be brought to bear against Salus."

"True, his poems are a little fusty. But people will come to appreciate them again someday. Like the furniture of our great-grandparents. Literature works in mysterious ways."

"Well, he does have one literary achievement to his credit," I said.

"And what would that be?"

"Salus, you know, is an obstetrician and gynecologist by profession. And in this capacity he assisted at my birth."

Brand burst out laughing. "Let me tell you something," he said. "I saw him not long ago at a lecture evening at the Club of German Women Writers. Yes, such a thing exists in Prague. I ended up there because someone sent me an invitation to a talk. You wouldn't believe how many female German writers there are in Prague. In the middle of the room was a big table piled high with countless novels, red clothbound Engelhorn editions. And in front of it stood these female writers, eagerly taking their pick, most of them probably dreaming of one day being published by Engelhorn themselves."

"You made that up, Brand."

"No, believe me! Every word is true. Adler also attended the lecture, actually more of a reading. First a young woman sang, 'From my great sorrows I make little songs,' accompanied by the piano. Then a poetess read a few of her poems — about a blind beggar, God, a Baroque park with cupid sculptures. Afterward Salus deigned to speak to me. 'Well, young poet,' he said, 'how did you like it?' What was I supposed to say? I answered with a question of my own: 'How did *you* like it?' 'I didn't much care for the one about God,' he said, 'but the poem about the cupids, I liked that one very much.'"

"Now that I believe," I interjected.

"Wait, I'm not finished yet. Adler joined in the conversation and said: 'Yes, these young poets! This new brood nowadays wouldn't dream of asking for advice anymore. Back in my day, I mean back in the old days, there was a literary pundit by the name of Klaar. Every one of us had to ask him first if a poem we wrote was publishable or not. But nowadays? The young generation? You think this Werfel would ever ask me if I think one of his poems was good or bad? And you're no different.'"

Brand and I both laughed.

"But that's not all," Brand went on. "Adler kept talking about the good old days. 'I knew another Prague writer,' he said. 'his name was Salomon Kohn. He was famous the world over, was even published by Reclam. He was so famous that once, in the small hours, someone knocked on his door, on Josefstädtergasse. Kohn opened. An American stood outside. Kohn asked: What do you want? The American answered: Nothing more. For now

I've laid eyes on Salomon Kohn. That was how they showed their respect to writers in the old days.'"

Brand had to stop, exhausted from speaking so much. He laughed and coughed at the same time. It was a little macabre, but I was happy that Brand had something to laugh about. The two literary pundits had meanwhile disappeared in the opposite direction, toward the Old Town Bridge Tower.

But we stayed on the bridge. On the other side, on the left bank of the Moldau, rose the acropolis of Hradschin, its evening lights already glimmering from the maze of roofs and houses in Lesser Town. In one of those houses, on old Radetzkyplatz, lived Brand.

The ground floor of the building consisted of open arcades, under which street vendors peddled their pottery, brooms and all manner of household goods. They were packing up their wares already, since it was almost dark. The giant, tightly locked iron-clad gate had a smaller door set into it, through which you entered into a musty, unilluminated passageway. This led to the courtyard, whose quadrangle was surrounded on all four sides by four floors of running balconies secured with iron railings, referred to in Prague as *Pawlatschen*, from the Czech *pavlač*, an echo of the *parvula loggia* found in Italian Baroque architecture. These balconies provided access to the apartments; the windows of the kitchens and the occasional other room looked out onto these *Pawlatschen*, which served as the setting for the building's gossip-mongering and where the shared lavatories of each floor were also located. It was one of those typical, ancient Prague buildings for people of "little means," an architectural monstrosity both cozy and eerie, the kind found haunting the stories and novels of Prague poets.

Branching off from the passageway before one entered the courtyard was the creaking wooden staircase with its steep, sagging steps leading to the upper floors, to the access balconies, to an incidentally inexplicable labyrinth of passages and corridors, and finally to the attics, where roof beams and laundry lines, junk and old crates went about their abstruse, surreal magic and, as we now know, exercised their own jurisdiction.

On one of the balconies Brand unlatched an apartment door and we entered a kitchen where, under a crucifix with an oil lamp, there stood an iron bed belonging to his sister, who wasn't home at the moment. Brand's room was behind this kitchen, adjoining his parents' bedroom. His father, a night laborer, had already left for work. His mother, not exactly small of stature but visibly bent by the burdens of existence, mutely attempted a welcoming smile. Then she left us alone.

Brand threw his cape over the bed. Fading twilight filtered through the *Pawlatsche* window and clung laboriously to the plaster head of a dusty-nosed Schiller on top of the wardrobe. From a bookcase with turned side posts Brand took a stack of manuscripts.

"Do you want to hear poetry or prose?" he asked in the midst of a raspy coughing fit that filled the room with a dreadful noise. And without even waiting for me to answer, as if he feared being hindered in his urgent need to read from his work, he immediately began reciting a poem from memory, waving the manuscript in his hand and pacing the room, so that the

Schiller head bobbed up and down or swayed to and fro, as if it were signaling applause or disapproval.

"Nothing but fever curves," he said at the end, dismissively, but obviously hoping I would protest, "just a graphic record of fevers. But I wanted to show you what my nights are like. Perhaps a doctor could make a diagnosis from them."

I mumbled some words of protest and praise. He sat down. It had meanwhile turned completely dark. "So here I am, dying away. A little like the student Ippolit in *The Idiot*, don't you think? There's nothing special about that. The remarkable thing is that I'm actually still alive, intensely and fiercely alive. And there must be some purpose in that. Take my father. He goes to work in the evening and comes back sometime in the morning. Then he goes to sleep. He gets up in the afternoon, eats and goes back to work again. *Telos!* Aim and purpose? Rent, food, medicines. Take my mother. You just saw her. She cleans people's houses, washes their laundry. Does it year in, year out. Aim and purpose? Rent, food, medicines. Take my sister, Marie. She's younger than me and, I think, is almost pretty. She slaves away the whole week. Sits in an attorney's office hunched over a typewriter, typing her fingers to the bone. What a wonderful life for a young thing like her! Aim and purpose? Rent, food, medicines. Our parents get all anxious if she buys herself a new dress now and then. Probably — hopefully — she's going out with some fellow. But she's never brought him home. It's because of me, I know it. My coughing might scare him off. They all work for my sake, because I'm the parasite eating up the money that could otherwise be put aside or used in a meaningful way. I lie there or crawl around, like some bug or beetle, good for nothing."

A violent fit of coughing interrupted Brand's speech, shaking his entire body before gradually transforming into a series of smaller coughs and eventually ceasing. "And yet," he continued, "there must be a reason for my existence, an aim and purpose, some worth, to justify the enormous amount of energy being spent on me. But the only meaning I see is what I write. There is no other. So what I write can't possibly be completely worthless. That would be perverse."

"Certainly," I blurted out, "and above all it's important for you." I was immediately taken aback by my own words, having restricted the importance of his work to himself. "And don't forget," I continued quickly, "that your family loves you. Would you not do the same for them?" I sensed immediately that I'd put my foot in my mouth again.

"So why did you publish some things of mine in your magazine?" he asked sharply. "Out of sheer pity?"

"Why on earth would you say that? I wouldn't publish a single line for that reason." I edited a small monthly magazine back then. It was supposed to promote the brotherhood of nations and publish cutting-edge poetry. It was wartime. We needed some humanity! But I would never publish a single line out of sheer pity.

"I wouldn't think so," said Brand. "And then there's Werfel. He also believes, or at least he said, that there's something about my work. But I wanted to ask *you* something. If, when I die, you could at least make a selection from my manuscripts and see that they get published. Just a small selection, so that something remains. Some meaning and purpose."

"Die? Why would you say that? Don't be such a pessimist. There are new treatments these days. Pneumothorax and . . ."

"They already tried that on me. No. It's useless. Sometimes I ask myself: Why am *I* condemned to die? I say that because of the cruel irony, the fact that I have this deep creative urge, as if someone wanted to make a mockery of me. If that weren't the case I could reconcile myself more easily. What a dreadful thought: my physical being, my earthly presence completely disappearing! Could you make sure that something remains?"

"I certainly will." The sentence dropped like a stone into the darkness of the room. I didn't dare add a consoling or hopeful word.

"Actually I wanted to read you something else, but I'll tell it to you instead. No need to turn the light on. It's easier to talk in the dark. I know it almost by heart." He paused for a moment to collect himself. Then he began, and these were his very own words:

"After twenty-one years of frail health Death ate into his lung and a raging fever seized him; he could feel his blood boil and the foam gathering on his lips. The white bed groaned under his wasted, shaken limbs. His blue eyes were veiled in a dull gray, thick veins bulged like ropes on his burning forehead, a mass of fire poured into his heart. I sit next to the sick man and hold his hand in mine. His voice broke at the first scream like thin, delicate porcelain and then sounded hollow, a rasping noise. His wrenching, wheezing cough cut through his squeaking throat, wandered around the room, bounced off the walls and faded away.

"His mother turned off the big bright light and lit a small, green flickering one — a lonely watchman over nights of suffering. I won't leave his bedside, I want to stay till morning, I point to the ottoman. The woman doesn't understand. The sick man lies there, sleep weighs down his burning lashes. His mother having left, the door closed without a sound. I see in a white bed, in the green light watching over the night, how he now opens his gray-veiled eyes and his gaze bores into mine; I feel, I know I'm imprisoned in his body, feel his pain, whistle his cough and sink into his sleep. I sleep but I'm awake. A thousand shapes shift ceaselessly under the green light. Outside it's raining, an endless drizzle. I'm awake in my sleep, aware of everything that is going on around me. Will this rain that ties me to this poky room and eats me up last forever? Will these clouds amassed in the sky ever go away? Do they want to obliterate the days with their endless flow of water, wash away everything bright from the streets? It's nighttime. From my feeble body, decaying with disease, a healthy one is born. I thus walk the streets with my new-born self. Everything is Self.

"The trickle of hours. Eternal hours, endlessly consumed. But the powers of the heavens are beginning to exhaust themselves. How refreshing it is, the rain easing up! Helplessly I walk through the blackness. Occasionally a tavern window gleams, but I don't hear a sound. The buildings seem alive inside, but their faces are dead. No sound, and everything inside me yearns for noises, sounds and words. The rain has died. I look around me in the darkness while I make my way forward. Oh, alien street, never walked by day and endless! Is this the street of death? The way is agonizing. A creature huddles on the tiles in the darkness of a doorway. I bend my head toward its face. A man without a nose, his left eye gone, his right one blindly fixed on the heavens, on his lap a concertina. The fingers are playing but the instrument makes no sound. I flee, the darkness hurts my eyes, a tremendous fear overcomes me that I myself could go blind. How many hours have I walked already? Or has it been minutes, and my fevered brain has turned it into hours?

"A black cat leaps from the ledge of a building, right over my feet and across the street. My eyes squint as they search for the nocturnal creature. I see it in the middle of the street, its black fur, usually soft, is now wet and shaggy. Its eyes burn and sparkle and mine are fixed on them. I stare into the fire of these eyes, until I hear a voice inside my head: Come! Follow me! I'll take you to where the ever-new rises from what has been, where wonderment will firmly seize you, in this phoenix-realm of eternal justice.

"I have no choice but to follow the animal, which moves backward like a crab. My gaze clings unwaveringly to these fiery eyes. It quickly leads me forward, I almost begin to pant, a strange whistling sound escapes through my teeth. I'm reeling from fatigue when the animal stops outside a house familiar to me from my dreams. I know this deserted house, whose windows are all bricked up and whose black iron gate seems like the sinister maw of Moloch. In its depths, way in the back, burns a flickering green hanging lamp that attracts me like a magnet. I climb the stairs. On every landing strange lamps are lit. Now I stand in the hallway of the top floor. I sense that someone is missing: the animal, the cat with the fiery eyes.

"I'm alone. The long hallway has no door. I seem to be trapped. I want to flee but can no longer find the stairs. I grope my way along the wall, lights shine from deep, empty eye sockets. Hours of groping. The palms of my hands are almost rubbed raw. My heart is wracked with fear. Then I finally find a door that leads to a dark chamber. It's round as a cauldron and in it is madly boiling blood, from which vapors rise. Life? I close my eyes.

"I awake again on an unknown street. I know it's daytime. I creep across the cobblestones, barely even moving. There's the house I live in. A procession departs from it. I see a black canvas board with white letters. The letters spell my name. They're burying me, and I stand here, alive. Two eyes open. I sit next to the sick man and hold his burning hand. I love him.

"But I know that soon he is going to die. His hand told me so."

This was a piece of Brand's legacy.

"That's how it's going to be," he said after a long silence. His mother entered, placing a little lamp with a green glass shade on the nightstand. While she did so, with unsteady hands, I saw her desperate gaze roving searchingly over her son, over me and the things in the room, before extinguishing in itself.

Wanda lived in a garçonnière with a tiny kitchen in what was then an ultramodern building in New Town. She worked as a kind of artisan. From different colored bits of fabric she created gay and fanciful hangings that mostly adorned her own walls and only rarely found a paying customer. Her male friend, the sharp-witted critic and bank clerk, covered her losses, even though she had never asked him for anything. She accepted what he gave, because she herself was used to giving. She was tall, energetic and trusted in life. Because of this trust in life, she showed no signs of egoism but was devoted and extravagant in everything she did. When she loved she knew no limits and was willing to commit every sin, venial or mortal. When she loved she let herself be loved and didn't make a fuss about it. But you couldn't get anything from her for money. "She doesn't know what six times nine is but can get through life just fine," Fürth used to say. He was only partly right. While she may not have known, she could guess how much six times nine is. Anyway, it was no big deal for her. She loved to swim, did gymnastics, and liked eating hearty meals, her slender, graceful figure never being the worse for it. Watching her sink her healthy teeth into a piece of roast and joyfully chew it to bits was a pleasure. For her, French cuisine was nothing but hocus-pocus, a bunch of phony-baloney. She herself was an accomplished cook. It was only to prove that she was capable of other things that she memorized pages of Kierkegaard, but in between she sang delightful Slovakian folksongs she'd learned from her mother, who hailed from the Tatras.

"You ought to read a few good books, the way they're meant to be read," I told her, cautiously beginning my diplomatic mission.

"Good books? But I do read good books. By Maupassant, for instance, or even by Marcel Prévost."

"That's not what I mean. Maupassant is very good, by the way. But you should read more systematically, so you really profit from it."

"When I read I don't *want* to profit from it. I want to be entertained, just like when I go to the theater. Awful, these complicated tragedies, Strindberg or whatever his name is. Oedipus! I've got enough troubles as it is. And you want me to listen to a story about some king who kills his father then sleeps with his mother, who then hangs herself, after which he gouges his own eyes out? The fellow who comes up with something like that ought to be taken to court."

"But you do, for example, read Kierkegaard."

"I've got my reasons. Besides, reading alone is boring."

That was the moment I'd been waiting for. "You're right about that. I think someone should read with you."

"What's that supposed to mean, you rascal? You don't need excuses to come here. I'm very fond of you. Why would you want to read with me? Let's go on an outing instead, to Karlštejn or Křivoklát Castle."

"Gladly. But I didn't mean with me. I meant with Brand. Brand is a wonderful reader and a very clever person. You could learn a lot from him."

Wanda's eyes opened wide. She was pouring tea into my cup and looked at me in disbelief, completely ignoring the tea, which was flowing over the rim and onto the lace doily.

"Would you look at this mess," she said. "You and your

Brand. Now I'll have to reset the table." I helped her clean up. "Brand is sick," she then said.

"Of course. He's sick. But he's a good person. He knows a lot. He's gifted. Werfel and Kafka say the same. His health could improve if someone looks after him. He would explain a lot of things to you, and besides it would strengthen his will to live. Soon you would know as much as Milena."

"Brand? I'm always afraid he's going to collapse right on the café table and die. And that hideous cough of his!"

"You shouldn't talk that way. Werfel wrote a poem about Jesus once:

But He His hair with little carrion bound,
A hundred corpses from His girdle hung,
His head with writhing wreath of serpents crowned,
Upon His shoulders bats and rodents clung."

"Ugh! You poets! Karl Kraus is right."

"Listen, Wanda. Jesus was not the first. Even the Buddhists . . ."

"I don't know a thing about Buddhists."

"You see, that's the trouble." I explained to her who the Buddhists were. "So even the Buddhists had a legend about a begging monk whom a leper once threw a bite to eat. And when he tossed it into the bowl a finger fell off with it."

"Will you stop it already. I'm not a begging monk."

"No. I won't stop. The begging monk wasn't disgusted at all, but ate the food. And in the end it goes:

Whoever has mastered this
is truly a citizen of the whole world."

"You're scaring me," said Wanda. "But I understand. As far as I'm concerned, Brand can come whenever he likes. Maybe it'll help him, maybe it'll help me. Does he even want to do this?"

"I think so," I said. "I think he really does."

Heinrich Mann had arrived but avoided any kind of welcome ceremony. He delivered his talk in a small meeting hall of the Palace Hotel. A tall, Art Nouveau-shaped floor lamp with a wide lace shade cast its pale light on his narrow, elongated à la El Greco face made even longer by the beard. We were so young that although he was well under fifty, to us he seemed ancient and nothing less than mythical. Cautiously and almost too softly, he spoke about the reasons for the demise of the Second French Empire, that it hadn't been war but the persistent signs of social decay that had brought about its downfall, since admittedly empires do not fall apart due to external causes but disintegrate from within, as a result of their many sins. It was hard to miss his allusions to the present and the profound warning contained in his words. The audience was mainly poets, writers and reporters.

Because in those days Prague, the city of the Golem, was still quite richly endowed with German-language authors. There were the curly-haired romantics and ragged realists, who'd been born around the middle of the previous century; the epigones of Rilke, who had journeyed into the unknown, their verse containing the muted echoes of Bohemian folksongs; the rhapsodists and apologists of the streetwalking daughters of pleasure in the manner of Toni the Gallows Girl, or Revoluce (as one of them was called who had fittingly set up shop in Café Parlament); and there were also the play-writing tenured professors at the Imperial and Royal Charles-Ferdinand University. And apart from the occasional lone wolf, who either stood his ground as a case *sui generis* or sank into oblivion, there was the circle that mainly met at Café Arco, where Brod espoused the primacy of the ethical over the purely formal, discovered poets and glorified the city, where they debated with genuine fervor "noble and ignoble misfortune," the "suffering of existence" and the "suffering of coexistence."

They were "Broding and Werfeling and Kafkaing and Kisching . . . !" as Kraus put it. But Aristophanic potshots lobbed from the beautiful blue Danube didn't hurt them all that much. We smiled at the red magazine that Headwaiter Poschta handed to us with compliments and that contained an ode entitled "Melancholy for Kurt Wolff," the publisher of the Expressionist avant-garde and the "Judgment Day" series, where more than one of us had appeared in print.

"From Orcus to Café Arco,
There, friends, lies posthumous fame, oh,
Published on the Day of Judgment."

Well then! Only the common descend into Orcus unsung, and that's all that matters. Those who are ridiculed have been faithful to the spirit, they've done their daily work, some of which has proved enduring. And even those poets who later fell silent still fulfilled their mission. For the world is nourished not only by triumphant minds but also by those who silently pass through it, not only by what achieves lasting fame but also by what is carried down on a daily basis into the vaults of deepest oblivion undisturbed by any fanfare.

Brand, as ever, was in the thick of it. He displayed a remarkable energy. Ever since he started visiting Wanda, he even began to look a bit better and cough a little less. Evidently he had found a way to manage his illness that offered him some external relief. To me his euphoria was dismaying. Because sometimes on our walks he would suddenly sigh, and his sighing sounded like prayers: "God, grant me patience! Give me self-control and trust! Give me firmness, leniency and assurance! Shelter me from fear!" Only someone who truly believed in God would be capable of making such demands on Him. Only someone who truly believed in God could express it so simply. God, to him, was not merely a form of invocation.

"I can see that He's there," he said. "How can a poet live without God? He's in the awareness of my inadequacy. In my knowing that nothing speaks in my favor while I nonetheless exist. In the fact that I recognize the flaws in my work, the wrongness of my ways, and yet still I write poetry, still I act. Imagine, I almost think I'm doing well. Of course, the fact that Wanda lets me visit her, that she pays any attention to me at all, can only be due to a certain shallowness. But in this, too, is God."

I asked Wanda about her meetings with Brand.

"Oh, we're reading Flaubert at the moment. It's called *Sentimental Education*. About this awful broad who won't let anything happen. But I told him a girl can't be like that, that it's utterly unnatural. He says it's wonderful and profound. But I say: where would we be if women were all like that? He brought me flowers. 'Don't be corny,' I told him. 'Flowers and candies, that's the kind of gift some old chairman of the board would bring. Read to me from your poems instead.' I'm not too interested in that either. But I can see it makes him happy. We also read something from Stendhal. But I'm afraid it won't last long. He's only human, and I'm just an average girl. It's no good when things aren't mutual."

"But now you're a very well-read young lady," I said.

"Well-read! He comes to see me three times a week now. A fine mess you've gotten me into. Serves me right for listening to you. I don't have the heart to turn him down. The first time he comes to see me, he sits down right across from me and stares at me for a while, doesn't say a word. 'Why are you staring at me like that,' I ask him, 'you never laid eyes on a woman before?' 'No,' he says, 'it's possible I haven't.' What am I supposed to do? I like it when the fellas fall in love with me a little. But you have to watch out. Especially with him. Well, if things get out of hand I can always just stick a cookie in his mouth. And then we'll read *The Red and the Black* or something like that."

"Has it gotten that bad?"

"Not really. He's very tactful. I promised him a wall hanging. He was very happy about it. I'm putting a forest on it, stylized of course, with a sun behind it. It's his as soon as I finish it. Sometimes I think I should try to get rid of him somehow, in a friendly way, and inwardly I curse you for foisting him on me. But other times he really moves me, because he really loves being alive and is looking better now and says it's because of me."

Wanda now joined the table talk at Arco more often than she used to. She no longer spoke in memorized quotes but made comments that smacked of an independent judgment. She would leaf through magazines and comment, say, on a poem: "Twaddle! An imagined feeling rather than a felt thought." Or she'd say: "What a hack! Uses adjectives like a life preserver." Clearly she was making progress. And such talk caused those who didn't know where it was coming from to sit up and take notice. Brand seemed pleased. The sharp-witted literary critic and bank clerk gave a tart, supercilious smile. For all intents and purposes, he'd long since cut himself loose from Wanda. He was simply waiting for the opportunity to replace her with a newer model, albeit a more impressive one, a woman over whom he and Kafka had long been waging a silent battle, one that Kafka would lose while still emerging victorious.

Kafka rarely came to the café. When he did he spoke in seemingly simple sentences. And yet they were the product of interminable preparations, a tangle of a thousand inner objections and scruples, rising from the blackest depths and which even his best friend, though undoubtedly the one with the deepest insight, was only cognizant of as a faint echo from the abyss. Behind his simple sentences was an unfathomable system of safeguards. Their syntax was illuminated by oblique rays of sunlight in which pygmies cast bizarrely giant shadows and giants were grotesquely dwarfed. He asked questions he answered himself in the form of other questions, in an almost

Socratic manner: "Don't you think that man is like a fisherman who doesn't really know for sure who's got hold of whom, if the fish has caught the fisherman or the fisherman the fish?" What he said seemed indisputable. He was, in the ordinary sense, neither right nor wrong. Being right or wrong is a privilege of the mediocre. Mere opinions can turn into idle chatter. His sentences stood like rocks; but rocks have a long history, arising from events occurring at fiery-molten or oceanic depths. He might then conclude with the simple words: "I'm learning. That's all."

And there sat Werfel, too. He sang of life with *flebile dolcezza*, the tearful sweetness of a troubadour. He, the friend of the world, also sang of futility, and of desperation great and small down to the distraught parlormaid who dropped the serving tray. Sang, too, of all-consuming self-doubt and sometimes shouted out: "My face is not yet my face, it is still the mask of my evasion. The actual struggle, with real and imagined devils, is only just beginning!" Sang nevertheless of heavenly glory and the rule of the stars, "draw, bear and hold a thousand smiling waters in your hand."

And there among them sat Brand, fevered and flushed, not just because he was sick but the way young people get during a theater performance. Because he (probably more than any of us) sensed in the glittering splendor of the coffeehouse chandeliers and the sparkling water glasses and cups and in the whirling movements all around him the singular intoxication of this spectacle, the curtains flying high, the prelude to the unforgettable, the vibrations of new-born metaphors and the drama of these two very different protagonists, as if the one were brandishing an inexhaustible horn of plenty and the other working tirelessly, despairingly on a grand edifice both unfinished and unfinishable, though withal rising above it with irony (which only underscored its being unfinishable).

Outside loomed the city of Prague, the old and the new, under the lingering smells of beer and smoked meats, with its Libuše legends, Hussite and other defenestrations, its alchemic vapors, the Golem's rampage, the more recent worlds of Neruda and Čapek, the oh-so ancient world of national strife, and the flowering gardens full of dreams and the undying strains of Mozart and Smetana.

The war, as I mentioned, did not affect the essence of the human events related here. But it did affect the people themselves, preying on their minds and spirits. It drove a wedge between table fellowships and national communities, pitting individuals against each other and driving them to the frontlines. Some came home on hurried furloughs. Some would never come back. They fell, some celebrated for their bravery, others bravely despairing, all equally lamentable. Of course, even without war we're the unintended witnesses of much internal and external decline, without which life seems unable to maintain its sovereignty. The macabre maelstrom of war, however, no matter how awful in its particulars, in the long run offered little more than a dreary picture of stagnation. Even this war, having begun with an ambitious clamor, eventually suffered the inevitable fate of a lethal and senselessly debilitating monotony.

One evening, arriving at home after a couple of months spent with a reserve unit of my regiment, I found a package in my room. It contained a few books I had lent to Wanda, a note and a rolled-up wall hanging depicting a forest and a sun. The note read as follows: "No Kierkegaard can help me, nor can *The Red and the Black*. Forest and sun are for Brand. I've got other plans."

It turned out that Wanda had fled, vanished, was simply no longer there. The sharp-witted critic and bank clerk had run off with Milena. This small and rather insignificant-looking man exuded an inexplicable basilisk-like magic, driving women into his arms who, whether of a simple or complicated nature, were apparently unable to resist him. In any case, Wanda had up and left. Fortunately she was healthy enough that I didn't need to worry about her. They said she had gone to Berlin, but no one knew for sure. Wanda would always find her way through life one way or another, even if she had to guess how much six times nine was.

I was much more worried about Brand. He had spent a long time in the hospital during my recent absence, then was sent home in a state of pernicious decline. I brought him Wanda's gift, and his sister and mother hung it up on the wall across from his bed. I paid him frequent visits. He had an untamable desire to talk, even though each word was a tremendous strain on him. I'll only recount our last meeting.

He lay there covered with one of those heavy, puffy Bohemian eiderdowns that heat you like a furnace. But it was obvious he was freezing. Manuscripts were lying on top of the bed. Some had fallen to the floor.

"He talks nonstop," whispered his mother, after escorting me into the room. "He's been doing this for three days and nights, and sometimes he screams so loud that everyone in the building can hear." She compulsively clasped and unclasped her hands. Brand didn't look at me when I entered. He stared at the wall hanging with forest and sun. But he knew I was there.

"I've been writing. Werfel heard me. Yesterday, no, must have been the day before. The days are starting to blur. Individual days no longer exist, just a single flow of time. He was with his white-haired female friend. How beautiful she is! But you've been here with him before. The woman's eyes are cool and clear as a forest pool. She has this way of walking, more like she's gliding on air. She always hovered past the windows of Arco."

A ghastly barrage of coughing interrupted each one of his fitful sentences. Occasionally these explosive eruptions made him sit up in bed. It was as if his body were the battleground of raging armies of bacteria now engaged in the decisive battle. His forehead shone yellowish and plastery like the Schiller bust on the wardrobe, which, Werfel said, seemed a gruesome parody of the sick man's emaciated face.

"Our dear Oskar Baum was here too. His wife brought him. 'I'm pleased to see you again,' he said. How funny! A blind man talks about seeing. But he did see me, better than I saw him. And he said: 'I see you've been writing a lot.'"

Brand's words came tumbling out, repeatedly interrupted by his cataclysmic coughing, which he galloped over like an apocalyptic rider with the sheer momentum of his speech.

"Humans aren't born into laughter, but amidst the wailing of their mothers. The pain of the woman in labor engraves itself in the body of the newborn and remains trapped inside it until death breaks it to pieces. But life is beautiful! Do you hear? Life if beautiful! What is hunger, thirst, pain? It's life and it's beautiful! It's the song of the light-winged. Falling in an arc, flying by. Cairo!"

He shouted the word "Cairo" three times in a row, as if it were a battle cry. I grabbed his hand from a need to calm him, but let it go again because it seemed to me that this gesture was for my sake or his mother's and that he shouldn't be hindered in his shouting and screaming.

The awful thing was that at this very moment some neighbors appeared on the balcony outside the window and looked into the room with horrified faces. His mother stepped up to the window and with a timid gesture shooed away the faces, which disappeared like clouds. Then she closed the curtain.

"Come! You're strong! Blessed art thou among women! You're rash and break me like a reed. She left. But he was there. Werfel! Sat there in his infinite love. Oh, farewell, fountain of all words! Life is beautiful! Somewhere on the front in the Eastern steppe it will suddenly hit him and he'll cry, ceaselessly: Life is beautiful! Is that my brain rattling? It's like an express train hurtling down the tracks. Where am I headed? Where's my ticket? I don't know the station anymore. I'll miss it."

He sat up suddenly and let out a piercing cry: "Cairo!" then sank back one last time.

The era, as far as there was one, slunk away like a shadow. The fiery tongues of the spirit came to only a select few. The friend of the world steered his bright comet's course in a southerly and westerly direction. Kafka's flickering star of contemplation was sinking into agony. I kept my promise. From afar the friend of the world sent his words of remembrance:

"Karl Brand, oh, poor dead man! Like all the dead beneath us, the vision of you has faded faster than the destruction wrought by putrefaction. So many fulsome years have passed, so many, unspeakably many have hastened through us with vigorous stride, and even memory proves powerless, that great necromancer, the only conjurer of the dead we have here on earth. I no longer see your face, cannot recall your features, in the distance hovers a pale, bluish fleck that doesn't have the strength to become a vision.

"Your legacy? The brief, gasping cry a breathless fugitive is allowed to utter when, crouching in a doorway, he believes himself to be safe for a while. Your work? A fragment on the great heap of broken shards of the murdered generations. Your strength? You're not alone.

"Uncanny eyes he had, the kind and bashful Brand, and uncanny, embittered eyes are what many of the twenty- and thirty-year-olds have who are incorruptible to the point of cynicism and so tormented by the big lie that they had to sacrifice beauty.

"They all know what they've been denied: the immortality that beckons only to the serene, the love that only the blissfully self-contained can reap, the happiness in life that only the joyfully, willfully deceived, that the believer alone attains. They gave this up. They themselves were given up on."

Years later I published a slim volume of Brand's poems and prose pieces. Werfel's words served as the introduction. My eulogy delivered at the funeral was the afterword. A quiet, already dying but eternally urgent voice later spoke the final blessing:

"Many thanks for the book. It reminded me very much of *Ivan Ilyich*, in its substance but also in its composition. First Werfel's very simple and terrible truth (true, also, about the uncanny, the joyfully, willfully deceived), then the death of this young man, the three days and nights of screaming, in reality one didn't hear a sound, and if it had been audible one would have moved a few rooms down, this is the only 'way out.' And finally your manly and comforting afterword, which of course one is all too eager to agree with, if only it didn't come too late, after the execution as it were, as is the nature of comforts. It is no different with Ivan Ilyich, only here in *The Legacy* it is even more pronounced, as every stage is particularly personified.

With cordial regards,

yours,

Kafka"

SUPERSTRUCTURE

The Magic Flute

Snow flurries in the city at night on the way home from a lighthearted gathering, I like that. I'll soon be lying under the covers, the snow will continue to blow against my windows, but when the lights are out I'll be playing "Gobi Desert," which always puts me to sleep. Gobi Desert is a dream game I invented, in which I drive a fantastic automobile through the deserts, across the oceans and through the skies. My car is equipped with everything needed for a comfortable life, it can transform at will into a ship or an airplane, is surrounded by an invisible and impenetrable wall through which no one can reach me unless I want them to. My journey begins in the Gobi Desert, I don't know why. But I never get very far, I see a couple of Bedouins or an oasis with drinking camels, and by then I usually fall asleep. Yes, that's what'll happen in a little while, what *could* have happened if no one had held me up.

I'm detained by a hunchbacked little man, who follows me through the snow and tugs at my sleeve. I'm vaguely familiar with him and his tugging, but this familiarity comes from a bygone era. "Don't you know who I am?" he asks. "I even owe you a debt of gratitude," he adds.

"What for?" I ask, "and in this foreign city, at that?"

"The city doesn't matter," he said. "You helped me out of a mess or two. I used to recruit the extras for crowd scenes in the theater. You cut a fine figure, especially in the opera." He gauged me with a shrewd eye. We were standing in the light of a streetlamp. "It's time I express my gratitude."

"On the contrary," I objected, "I'm the one who should be thanking you. If you'd like, come up to my place for a while. Otherwise, I lack for nothing at the moment."

"If it were possible," cried my hunchbacked little man — it really was him, the recruiter of extras — "if it were possible to lack for nothing. Allow me nonetheless to take you to the opera."

"You're joking," I said. "It's well past midnight, and the theater closed a long time ago."

"Not at all," he contradicted, "the show, in fact, hasn't even begun."

I can't explain why suddenly the ancient car was there that looked like a stagecoach. He opened the door, at any rate. With imperious affability he motioned me to get in, sat down at the wheel himself and drove the car downtown. And although it was rather far, he negotiated the snow-covered streets with surprising speed so that in a matter of minutes we had reached the vast square where the building stood with its busts of the great masters above the portico and the horn-playing Polyhymnia above the pediment.

"You see," I said triumphantly, "it's completely dark and deserted."

"You're mistaken," muttered the recruiter, pushing me up the broad flight of steps to the middle doorway. From his coat pocket he took a small key, and to my great astonishment he opened the door, noiselessly and with ease.

"What are we supposed to do in there, all alone and in the dark?" I asked. It gave me the creeps, and I cursed my willingness to go along with everything, which time and again had gotten me mixed up in the countless adventures comprising a good part of my life.

In response the little man flipped a switch and immediately the foyer was bathed in radiant light. I found myself in the midst of a throng of figures, ladies with bare shoulders, cavaliers in full dress, liveried servants.

The little man cleared a path through the crowd and up the bright marble steps with red carpet runners until we reached the first balcony. There he entrusted me to a peculiar box attendant. "Fräulein Schikaneder," he said offhandedly, "loge 'zero' for the gentleman." Then he turned to me. "You'll have to excuse me now. Gala performance, the last of the season. *The Magic Flute* with a load of extras. But I'll see you at the end." And with these words he left.

"Oh, loge zero," said the attendant, respectfully yet grinning. I say she was peculiar because she didn't look at all the way a box attendant normally does, nor was she dressed like a staff member. She was youthful, even downright charming. She wore a trailing gown which fanned out in festive folds, and a dainty bunch of keys on her hip seemed to indicate her function. She opened the little door for me, and I entered.

There it was again, the familiar red-gold auditorium, the giant, umbel-like chandelier with its iridescent glass prisms and glittering crystals hovering in the middle, giving off millions of vibrating, shattering reflections. The curtain was there too, with its colorful allegory of the Muses descending from Parnassian heights, Thalia in the lead. From her hips flowed a heraldic ribbon in a noble, meandering curve down to the prompter's box. Above the loges swayed golden, mirror-bearing cupids.

The parquet rustled with a well-dressed, self-confident throng. Some sent nonchalant greetings up to the boxes, less to actually greet anyone than to express their intimacy with their occupants, who for their part waved back with an emphatic and therefore shallow affability. From the orchestra seats, the existence of the balcony not to mention the gallery was lost in an indefinite and hazy beyond. But the fairytale land of my youth was located in this very haze. The whole auditorium simmered with the jumble of a thousand conversations and greetings, with the flipping-through of programs, the crackle of candy bags, and the cascading sounds of instruments being tuned and tested by the musicians.

My wanting a concert program seemed like a suitable pretext to keep an eye out for my lovely attendant. I spotted her in the narrow walkway running along the boxes just as the bell began to ring.

"You should come sit with me in the box," I told her by way of invitation, "at least during the performance."

"No, no," she whispered, "what would the manager say?"

"The manager has more important things to do."

She looked at me uncomprehendingly. "But what about the stage manager!"

"I know him personally." That was a lie, but it was true that in elementary school I did know the son of a stage manager by the name of Gomolka, which is why he called himself Körner. "Besides, I'm the guest here and can invite whomever I want."

She resisted for a while, saying "I couldn't possibly," but eventually gave in, as was to be expected, and scurried into the box with me.

The instruments, now warmed-up, fell silent. The murmur of the audience subsided. The chandelier went out. It was dark like before the creation of the world. Down in the orchestra pit a spotlight suddenly fell on the hawk-nosed conductor. He raised his hand. His finger described an arc, parted the fog, put the elements in their place.

Then he tapped his baton, two terse, dry whacks of indescribable sobriety. Inconceivable how such a dispassionate tapping can be followed by the mighty calls and enchanting garlands of the overture. Then the colorful curtain of Muses was lifted, the gray velvet traveler curtain was swept away to both sides, and the wildly flowering island dream with fairytale palms and tangles of lianas opened up before us. And in came the handsome young man, pursued by a serpent and singing for help. Oh, Burian, Winkelmann, Slezak, Schmedes, your voices so divine!

"This portrait is bewitchingly beautiful!" Rise, you faithful lovers. "Can this sensation be love?" Spring, summer, fall and winter, gallery, balcony, orchestra and loge, yes, yes, It can only be love. Auditorium and stage, no one knows who's there for whom. And all around, in countless offices, the infinite directorship of Angelo Neumann is at work. Forever and always it is and remains the work of Angelo Neumann. He stands there, a giant, and cries: "Before there was Teweles there's me!"

On stage, the glittering empress of the night now let her coloraturas gush forth. Virile wisdom emerged from brown twilights. World-weary infatuation sang in a gold-blonde soprano. We know that type, I said, curled up behind all the store counters of the world. We say "shop" here, my box companion interjected. Fine, behind all the shop counters of the universe. And who should come along then with a village ditty? The Sancho Panza or Super-Švejk of the opera and the literary world, provoking raucous laughter, he's the bird-catcher after all. Don't poke your nose in other people's family affairs.

The curtains closed. Certain members of the audience held their hands behind their back to indicate they would never ever applaud no matter how much they liked it, since they had to show they were used to far better performances. The audience rose like a wave from their seats. The intermission had begun. "I'll be going now," said my loge companion. "But you'll come back," I called out after her.

I went to the balcony foyer, where people gathered during intermissions. Shadows, fragrant and elegant, crowded around the two buffets, sat at tables, stood and strolled around. Friends and acquaintances greeted and waved to me as if they had seen me just yesterday. They seemed unaged and unchanged. Had I long become part of their afterlife without my even knowing it?

At one of the tall arched windows the delicate harpist of prose stood gazing out into the darkness glimmering here and there with snow. He wore the smile of the Tenean Apollo, a mixture of wonder and melancholy, irony and foreboding. As always and in the days of old, there was an empty space around him, a magic circle. I wondered if I might manage to approach him, cross the invisible barrier. But doing this would have meant saying something infinitely simple and utterly true. "Opportunities of this sort are few," he noted, divining my thoughts.

Propped against a column, seemingly wrapped around it like some exotic vine, was a gaunt fellow with a protruding chin, a shiny black forelock and a monocle. He was entertaining a gaggle of younger shadows with his droll anecdotes. As if from a machine gun, he rattled off entire volleys of punchlines, eliciting incessant explosions of laughter. There seemed to be no end of things to laugh about.

A number of aristocrats from nowhere roamed the room, either overlooked by or eluding the grasp of Mirabeau; then the angular engineer and architect types with their dopey stares, horn-rimmed glasses and starched shirts; the jewel-laden wives of bank directors; editors whose gestures showed just how much they knew everything better; professors striving to shake off from their burdened brows the weariness of entirely forgotten peoples; young ladies with searching eyes (you girls are like boats, says Rilke, moored to the shores of the hours). Everyone spoke of music. "You must always bear in mind, madam, that, while music flows in a straight line through time, its presence is spatial, filling all dimensions simultaneously. And this simultaneity of the longitudinal and spatial, of spiritual and corporeal reality, that's the secret of music," someone said, biting into a lobster-salad roll. "But," said another shadow, "how can it be that the music is beautiful, the voices magnificent, yet I don't understand a single word, don't even recognize the language it's being sung in. Is that not a misuse of words, of language, of ideas and concepts, content and form?" — "Who is that, anyway?" asked a shadow at a marble table. "Who could it be?" said another, "I don't know him." "Yes, who could it be?" said a third shadow, "I sat with him in the coffeehouse for years." "And why," said the voice from before, "don't they simply sing in bird language or the language of slowworms, which, according to the forest goats, sounds beautiful and sweet?"

Under the trumeau mirror I suddenly recognized the poet. He was sitting with the young actress whose eyes shone like moonstones and were therefore so perilous, because when they looked at you, you stopped thinking altogether.

"How did you get here?" he called out to me. "I thought you were sitting comfortably in the train of time."

"I don't know if I'm awake or dreaming," I said.

"Both, my dear fellow," he answered, "both. It's always like that. And then some. Your former self, current self and future self always coexist. That's the eternal trinity." He spoke with verve, and all of it was said for the shiny-eyed goddess sitting next to him. He was only using me as a foil, I sensed. But when do poets ever speak to people as individuals? Not even to their shiny-eyed goddesses.

A loud ringing cleared the many shadow figures from the foyer; by the time I reached box zero the lights in the auditorium had dimmed and the second act was underway. The young lady was back. She was sitting on the red plush bench at the back of the box. I went straight for her hand, took it and said:

"Schikaneder. Yes, you really did exist at this theater. I'm neither dreaming it nor is it poetic license. I saw you often. And they always told me you actually were descended from the family of the famous librettist. Back then, though, you looked completely different. In those days you were, pardon my saying so, already pretty old."

"And how," she said in good spirits. "I've given myself a little makeover. It's easy to do over here. Over there you live on borrowed time. By the way, you're very rude, apart from which you're keeping me from listening."

"Oh, come on, surely you know each bar by heart."

"Let's say: each line. Yet still I'm always hearing it for the first time. And each time I get angry all over again."

"Why should you get angry? Is the music not divine?"

"You talk just like all the others. Of course the music is divine. But no one is listening to the words. Sometimes I wish the lyrics would rebel a little."

"The lyrics, the lyrics! All due respect for your great-great-grandfather. But ultimately it's the music that matters."

"Unbelievable! And why did old Goethe — you've probably heard of him — why did he plan to write a sequel? And did he succeed? My forebear from Straubing knew damn well what he was doing, even if his magic island borrowed a bit from Wieland. My forebear was a rebel. 'The Enlightenment is on the march,' he said. 'We'll show them,' he said. And who the Queen of the Night was, everyone in Vienna knew that. But then a hundred and fifty years intervened and people only listened to the music, even though Mozart knew exactly why he was knocking on doors in E-flat major and unleashing the trombones and woodwinds and harmonizing them with the flute and rattling the bells. But old Schikaneder, he's allowed to die in a madhouse, and his libretto, they say, is stupid. Which of course means that, unwittingly, they're saying Mozart is stupid too. They, these gentlemen and ladies, think they're all so incredibly smart."

She was lovely delivering her grand speech. I sealed her mouth with a kiss. But I was suddenly torn from the depths of this kiss by the highly unexpected things now taking place on stage below.

The two men in armor suddenly stepped up to the apron and struck up a completely unanticipated antiphony, their words bursting forth with growing force: "We demand . . . We demand!" What they were demanding was more or less unintelligible. But it didn't sound like Mozart. They weren't on their own for long. Two priests from the Temple of Wisdom soon joined them and sang in a swelling chorus: "We demand . . . We demand!" From the wings flitted the lascivious Moor and shrieked as if he were a thousand Moors: "We demand . . . We demand!" The three ladies pranced, the three boys hopped in a sextet: "We demand . . . We demand!" The bird-catcher was also there, together with his little woman; the ministering spirits of the noble halls, the court of the Midnight Queen, in short: all the extras streamed on stage, even the handymen, the scene-shifters, the curtain-pullers, the wardrobe mistresses and cloakroom attendants, the firemen, the ticket-takers, the box-office girl, the doorman Podlesný along with his family, in the end even the lighting technicians, who cried out: "Kotulan is waiting in vain!" — he was the lighting chief — and everyone, everyone multiplied a hundredfold, in fugues and counter-fugues, the incessant cry of "We demand . . . We demand!"

Down in the orchestra pit the hawk-headed conductor tried to go on conducting Mozart, but the music grew thinner and thinner, as one by one — like the Haydn symphony that trails off — the musicians got up and left, joining the chorus of demanders on stage. A shudder swept over the gallery and parts of the balcony. But in the orchestra seats people remained where they were, seemingly unaffected.

"They still haven't noticed a thing," said Frl. Schikaneder.

No, they didn't seem to notice anything, which is why what I had been vaguely fearing for years was now probably bound to happen. It began with a deep sigh, coming, as it were, from a secret dungeon. I saw the big chandelier gradually start to sway, describing ever bigger circles and nearly grazing the upper gallery. Then, as if it had abruptly changed its mind, the chandelier, defying every law of physics, suddenly returned to the middle, where it hung vertically and motionless and apparently ready to concede another second-long respite; then its thousand bulbs flared up, spilling blinding cataracts of light into the auditorium for a moment before going out — and then, silent and terrible, the hulking thing came hurtling down.

The stage was still fully lit, and those with eyes to see might have glimpsed the colorful Egyptian scenery, the same set, by the way, that was used for *Aida*. The mighty crowd up there, having just intoned its powerful "We demand . . . we demand!" now stood rigid and mute, as if afraid of itself. From below came groaning and wailing, hissing and howling, the gnashing of teeth; from the stage an unsteady light flickered over the unbridled panic of frantic tailcoats and décolletés. But over the rocket screams of horror and the croaking basses of despair one heard the offended falsettos of personal indignation.

The iron curtain slowly began to descend, but failed to close completely. The flames of the burning scenery kept licking at the dusty curtains of the proscenium boxes. The gilded cupids came loose from their frames, dropped their mirrors and zigzagged wildly through the auditorium. The prompter's box melted and flowed into the orchestra pit, where the instruments, left to their own devices, ripped and raged as they took on fantastic Picasso-like shapes.

A girl with bare breasts glided down from the railing of the gallery, didn't fall, no: floated obliquely, drifted like a blossom and vanished into the depths. In the neighboring box two men gestured. "It's your fault!" — "What do you mean, my fault, I wanted masked lighting right from the start. You insisted on the chandelier!"

Frl. Schikaneder introduced me: "The architects, Messrs. Fellner and Helmer." Both gentlemen bowed respectfully.

Through the gap that was left in the iron barrier one could see the painted curtain falling at an angle, as if it had come loose on one side. The blaze devoured it. The bodies of the colorful Muses curled up in the flames, shrinking and being reduced to ashes in the frenzied fire.

"My oh my," remarked Frl. Schikaneder, "it's all being destroyed again!" She was expressing more her surprise than horror.

"Look how you're behaving," I shouted angrily. "You act as if none of this means anything to you. But me, all my blooming hopes have been dashed, all the divine melodies have vanished, all the glories of the world are going up in smoke, Orpheus and Don Giovanni, Pavlova and Duse, Caruso and Kainz! Never again will you hear the radiant fanfare of his voice, my friends! Time is out of joint! Help us, Oedipus, help us, King!"

"How nicely you sing the twilight," said the lady dreamily and took my hand. With gentle coercion she led me out of the box down seemingly endless dark and narrow, winding emergency stairs to a little door and pushed me through. Something clanked shut behind me, between her and me, forever. I stood in the middle of the old theater garden, where the little recruiting agent was waiting for me. He took me by the arm and we trudged through the snow in silence for a while.

"It's astonishing," he said, "how people have got tons of kitsch hanging over their heads and consider things permanent which, according to the law of appearances, can never last."

"If I understood you correctly," I said, "you were trying to do me a favor?"

We were standing in the halo of a streetlamp.

"Well, I did what I could," said the little man, "It's not the dream that needs to be interpreted. It's the dream itself that interprets. You'll soon be under your covers. The snow will whip against the windows, and you'll start playing Gobi Desert. But no matter how far you go, you'll always come back with your caravan of dreams, revisiting the old stages, the vanished orchestras, the long since deserted auditoriums, you'll sing and play all the roles, be director, conductor and first violin, as the audience you'll applaud, as a hurtling chandelier smash everything to pieces — and you'll never abandon the dream until its interpretation is complete."

"And when will that be?"

"In the north of India," the little man answered, "there exists an old shrine, above whose doorway the windblown words of the Lord have come to rest: Jesus, on whom be peace, once said: The world is a bridge; pass over it, but build no house upon it."

The snow swept the little man away like a flake. I saw him swirl past the streetlamp, which swayed in the wind and circled high above my head.

NOTES

31 The Friend of the World *and* One Another: *Der Weltfreund* (Berlin: Axel Juncker, 1911), Franz Werfel's debut collection of poetry, and *Einander. Oden, Lieder, Gestalten* (Leipzig: Kurt Wolff, 1915), a collection of his Expressionist poetry.

31 Tycho Brahe *and* Reubeni: Two popular historical novels by Max Brod: *Tycho Brahe Weg zu Gott* (Kurt Wolff, 1915); *Reubeni, Fürst der Juden* (Kurt Wolff, 1925).

40 *Calve's, the old bookshop:* in 1790 Jan Bohumír Calve established a bookshop and publishing house for German and Czech language books that was located on Malé náměstí.

67 *an essay on me in English:* Werfel's "Weissenstein: World Reformer" (*Free World*, 1942).

79 *the great Expressionist publisher:* Kurt Wolff Verlag, founded in Leipzig in 1913 with Werfel serving as editor until 1915.

79 Action *and* Storm . . .*:* respectively, *Die Aktion*; *Der Sturm*; *Saturn*; *Aufschwung*; *Die Sichel*; *Die Flöte*; *Die Rote Erde*; *Das neue Pathos*.

81 *Herr Pollak, the bank clerk:* Ernst Pollak (1886-1947) was a Jewish German-language literary critic, author, and translator in a bank (referred to below as Herr P. and "sharp-witted"). A prominent figure in the Prague Circle, he was a regular at Café Arco, where he met Milena Jesenská, later marrying her. And as

an early champion of Franz Kafka's work, he was the one who introduced him to Jesenská.

84 Piquant World: *Pikantní svět*, a Czech humor magazine from the early 20th century, at times mildly erotic.

85 *the victorious revolution:* On October 28, 1918, the independent Czechoslovak Republic was declared and the National Council assumed power in what was less a revolution than a bloodless transfer of power that brought to a close centuries of Habsburg rule. Since the Marian column was viewed as a symbol of the recatholicization brutally imposed by the Habsburgs after the Battle of White Mountain, it was pulled down by a mob.

89 *Karl Brand:* (1895-1917), German-language poet who died of tuberculosis at the age of twenty-one. His short "sequel" to Kafka's *The Metamorphosis*, in which the insect Gregor Samsa ends up on a rubbish heap and transforms back into a human, appeared in the *Prager Tagblatt* in 1915.

99 *Walter Fürth:* (1891-1942), along with Karl Brand and Urzidil, part of the younger generation of Prague writers frequenting Café Arco, which is where he introduced Urzidil to his future wife, Gertrude Thieberger. She remembered Fürth as "a remarkable man, highly intelligent, sharp, educated . . . but so lazy he wrote only the beginnings of novels, just the opening sentence, which does require considerable talent."

163 *Bezruč's* Silesian Songs . . . *and Březina's* Mysterious Distances: Petr Bezruč, *Slezské písně* (1909); Otokar Březina, *Tajemné dálky* (1895).

175 The Legacy of a Young Man: the posthumous collection of Karl Brand's writing, *Das Vermächtnis eines Jünglings*, ed. by Johannes Urzidil, Preface by Franz Werfel (Vienna, Prague, Leipzig: Verlag Eduard Strache, 1921).

177 *"Man is spirit . . .":* and passages below in Søren Kierkegaard, *Fear and Trembling and The Sickness Unto Death* (Princeton: Princeton University Press, 1941), trans. Walter Lowrie.

178 *blind Oskar Baum:* (1883-1941), a Jewish German-language novelist and music critic who lost his sight in childhood. He became close friends with Max Brod and Franz Kafka.

178 *a tall female figure with snow-white hair:* Alma Mahler (1879-1964), who married Werfel (her third husband) in 1929, having started a relationship with him while still married to Walter Gropius, whom she divorced in 1920.

180 *the daughter of a Bohemian factory owner:* Heinrich Mann's first wife was the Jewish Czech actress Maria "Mimi" Kanová.

181 *at Milena:* Milena Jesenská (1896-1944), celebrated Czech journalist famous for her correspondence with Franz Kafka, was a habitué of Café Arco, and because this and her liaison with Ernst Pollak was considered erratic behavior, her father had her committed to an asylum in 1917 on grounds of "moral insanity." She had herself released nine months later.

196 "But He His hair . . .": In Franz Werfel, *Poems* (Princeton: Princeton University Press, 1945), trans. Edith Abercrombie Snow.

198 *Toni the Gallows Girl:* The heroine prostitute of the 1921 "literary reportage" *Die Himmelfahrt der Galgentoni* by Egon Erwin Kisch. More commonly known as "Tonka of the Gallows" from the 1930 Czech film adaptation *Tonka Šibenice.*

198 *the red magazine:* The satirical magazine *Die Fackel* [The Torch] edited and largely written by Karl Kraus from 1899 to 1936 and known for its iconic red cover.

204 *had run off with Milena:* Soon after marrying Ernst Pollak in 1918 against her parents' wishes, Jesenská absconded with him to Vienna. Pollak proved to be an inveterate philanderer and their marriage ended in divorce seven years later.

212 *the vast square where the building stood:* the Prague State Opera on Wilsonova Street, originally the New German Theater, with Angelo Neumann serving as director from its opening in 1888 until his death in 1910.

GLOSSARY OF PLACE NAMES

Aussig: Ústí nad Labem
Baumgarten: Stromovka Park (Královská obora)
Bergmannsgasse: Havířská ul.
Bohemian Forest: Šumava
Eisengasse: Železná ul.
Emperior Franz I Bridge: later renamed Most Legií (Legion Bridge)
Graben: Na Příkopě
Hibernergasse: Hybernská ul.
Hradschin: Hradčany
Josefstädtergasse: formerly Josefská ul., now Široká
Karlsplatz: Karlovo náměstí
Karolinenthal: Karlín
Kastulusgasse: Haštalská ul.
Kleiner Ring: Malé náměstí
Kohlmarkt: Uhelný trh
Königgrätz: Hradec Králové
Krakauergasse: Krakovská ul.
Kuchelbad: Malá Chuchle
Langengasse: Dlouhá ul.
Lieben: Libeň
Melantrichgasse: Melantrichova ul.

Melnik: Mělník
Moldau: Vltava
Oberplan: Horní planá
Obstgasse: Ovocná ul. (currently Ulice 28. října)
Obstmarkt: Ovocný trh
Olmütz: Olomouc
Pardubitz: Pardubice
Pilsen: Plzeň
Platteis: Platýz Passage
Potschaplitz: Počaply
Radetzkyplatz: Malostranské náměstí
Café Radetzky: Malostranská kavárna (presently a Starbucks)
Rittergasse: Rytířská ul.
Teyngässchen: Týnská ulička
Trautenau: Trutnov
Tschaslau: Čáslav
Waldsteinplatz: Valdštejnské náměstí

PUBS

Bigalsky's: U Bigalských (corner of Jindřišská ulice, defunct)
Black Brewery: Černý pivovar (House of the Golden Lion on Karlovo náměstí, defunct)
Flek's: U Fleků
Glaubitz's: U Glaubiců
Pinkas: U Pinkasů
Primates': U Primasů
Schnell's: U Schnellů

JOHANNES URZIDIL (1896-1970) was a writer, poet, historian, and journalist. Born in Prague, he was the youngest member of the Prague Circle, later penning the collection of essays *There Goes Kafka*. When Nazi Germany occupied Bohemia and Moravia in 1939, he and his wife, Gertrude (née Thieberger), the daughter of an Orthodox rabbi, first fled to England before later moving to the United States, becoming American citizens. He started publishing fiction later in life, and is perhaps best known for the story collections *The Lost Beloved* and *Prague Triptych*. Urzidil won a number of awards for his writing, including the Grand Austrian State Prize, and has an asteroid named after him. He died of a stroke in Rome while on a lecture tour of Italy.

DAVID BURNETT, a native of Cleveland, Ohio, has lived since the mid-1990s in Leipzig, Germany, where he works as a translator. He was a 2018 Translation Fellow of the National Endowment of the Arts (NEA) and received a 2014 PEN/Heim Translation Fund grant for his work on Johannes Urzidil's stories, which include the collections *The Last Bell*, *House of the Nine Devils*, and *Prague Triptych*.

PRAGUE TRIPTYCH
by Johannes Urzidil

Translated by David Burnett from the original German
Prager Triptychon, published in 1960 by
Albert Langen — Georg Müller Verlag, Munich

Cover image reprinted from the Collection of the
Museum of Prague with permission

Layout and design by Silk Mountain

Text set in Garamond Premier Pro

FIRST EDITION

Published in 2026 by
Twisted Spoon Press
P.O. Box 21 — Preslova 12
150 00 Prague 5
Czech Republic
www.twistedspoon.com

Printed and bound in the Czech Republic by Tiskárna PROTISK, s.r.o.

To promote sustainability and the responsible use of resources,
this book is made from Forest Stewardship Council® certified paper.

Distributed to the trade by
CENTRAL BOOKS
www.centralbooks.com

SCB DISTRIBUTORS
www.scbdistributors.com